SEVEN SEALS

Shot seven times, twice in the head, Lisa Hanley should be lying on a slab in the morgue, but she has cheated death and her family want revenge, not only for her attempted murder, but also for the theft of the cash she was carrying. Detective Louis Burrows has not witnessed such violence in a long time and knows the attack has all the markings of a gangland hit, and he knows there will be reprisals. Is the Mafia linked to Lisa's attempted murder, and will the streets of New York once again be bathed in the blood of gangland brothers?

SEVEN SEALS

SEVEN SEALS

by

Victor Headley

Magna Large Print Books
Long Preston, North Yorkshire,
BD23 4ND, England.

British Library Cataloguing in Publication Data.

Headley, Victor
    Seven seals.

    A catalogue record of this book is
    available from the British Library

    ISBN   0-7505-1997-5

First published in Great Britain in 2002 by Hodder & Stoughton
A division of Hodder Headline

Copyright © 2002 by Victor Headley

Cover illustration by arrangement with
Hodder & Stoughton Ltd.

Published in Large Print 2003 by arrangement with
Hodder & Stoughton Ltd.

Magna Large Print is an imprint of Library Magna Books Ltd.

Printed and bound in Great Britain by
T.J. (International) Ltd., Cornwall, PL28 8RW

This story goes to Claudia from the Wailers bus and all the sisters, mothers and daughters whose gentle wisdom soothes our tempestuous souls and feeds our elusive dreams.

Prologue

Seven bullet wounds. Two of them to the head. One of the slugs had gone right through the left upper jaw and come out on the other side of the face. The two kids searching the scrapheap got so scared on coming upon the bloodied and broken-up body that had been dropped from the bridge that they fled. They came back with an older boy who, after a quick look, decided the woman was dead but called an ambulance anyway. (In this part of town, no one ever called the police, even anonymously...) Yet when the paramedics lifted her up and placed her in the wagon they heard a muffled whimper filter out of her smashed mouth. While the driver sped away from the notoriously unsafe neighbourhood, the other did his best to clean her up and strapped an oxygen mask to her face. Even the most seasoned surgeons were shocked that someone having suffered such extensive injuries could still be alive. They didn't think there was much hope she'd survive but they operated on the young woman all the same, because that is what being a doctor is all about; you try to save lives even when the odds of survival are almost next to none. But survive she did...

Sunday Night

'We're wasting our time here, Ray. She's lost almost half of her blood, the left lung is gone ... and even if she makes it, the last bullet is much too close to her brain. She'll be a zombie.'

'The monitor's ticking, right? We go on and try to keep it that way.'

Above the mask, Bobby's eyes searched Ray's. Over the past year he'd been working with the senior surgeon he had learned to trust his judgment. Yet this time he seriously doubted the young woman laying unconscious on the table with tubes sticking from her mouth and chest could stand it.

'She's too weak to stand any more for now,' he said.

A nurse stretched and mopped sweat drops from Ray's brow.

'That slug gets loose and it's all over... Let's do it.'

Bobby nodded, took a breath before picking a new scalpel from the tray...

In the scrubbing room, they removed their

soiled green clothes, washed in silence and left together. The coffee in the almost deserted staff canteen was hot and bitter. On a table at the back, near the drink dispenser, a young nurse was napping, head resting on her hands.

'You know, Bobby, it's a long time I ain't seen someone damaged that bad and still breathing. I wonder who could have done her like that.'

Bobby sipped and shrugged. Stout and swarthy, he looked more like a Lebanese bar owner than a surgeon.

'I heard they found her on the East Side. It's a real psycho's nest down there.'

One bite of the doughnut convinced Ray it wasn't worth eating. He stretched his weary legs, slicked back his greying hair with both hands.

'Yeah... Sometimes I feel we're working in a partnership with them: they wreck 'em, we mend 'em!'

'They must be worried we'd become unemployed if they stopped.' Bobby said, shaking his head with a mirthless grin.

Dark humour like this was suitable only for surgeons like them – men who spent their days and nights wallowing in guts and blood, taking hours trying to fix the damage done in only a few seconds.

'You ever thought of doing something else, Bobby?' Ray asked.

They'd been working together since Bobby had arrived from back west with his newly acquired degree and laid-back ways. At first, Ray had thought he was just one of those spoiled kids from a rich family in search of a meaning for his life, like a few he'd come across in his thirty-year career. The recommendation he'd arrived with was just too good to be true. But he had been happily surprised and relieved: Bobby was genuinely gifted and hungry to learn.

'Well, my first love was really forensic medicine.'

Ray squinted at the younger man.

'You're kidding, right?'

'Nope, I wanted to be Quincy ... you know?' Bobby answered seriously.

'Hmm… It's not too late. The day you get tired of those still alive, you can always ask for a transfer to the other side. It's a little quieter down there ... and you won't have to worry about watching the monitor no more.'

Bobby made a face and downed the rest of his black coffee in one gulp.

Tuesday

The staff nurse was large, black and sullen looking. Whether she had a personal dislike of Detective Burrows or hated all policemen alike he couldn't tell, but she had never had a kind word for him in all the years of their uneasy professional relationship. 'Betsy', her colleagues called her, but she had coldly pointed out to Burrows that 'Miss Watts' was the way he should address her. This morning was a bad one for Louis Burrows. His estranged wife had called to cancel his visit with their only daughter, this despite the clear instructions set out by the family court. Burrows was smarting at this, especially because he knew it was just spite on the part of the woman. Three years after their divorce, his ex-wife still couldn't manage to sustain a relationship, so every time someone finally ran out on her, she did her utmost to take it out on him. He had to suffer because she suffered, that was the way it looked to him. It made Burrows angry that she'd invented a reason to stop him from taking Charlene out for the weekend, but then he just couldn't take the hassle of wasting his morning going through the motions in court. And now Miss Watts seemed determined to make his day even more miserable.

'Look, you know the procedure: an injured person gets brought here, you file a report to the station, I come here to get details about it. I know you're very busy and so am I, so why don't we make it easy on ourselves and do this nice and quickly?'

Weary as he felt, Burrows tried a smile, just in case it would make a difference. It didn't.

'And I tell you once more that we don't know anything about that one – nothing, nada. She got brought in two days ago barely alive. Got shot seven times, that's all I know.'

'How about a name?'

'No name.'

'Anything on her, in her pockets...?'

'No pockets.'

'Anything particular on her body – tattoos, scars, marks ... anything.'

'Marks? Yeah: seven, made by metal objects. Bullets we call them.'

'Very funny!'

'Right. Now if you'll excuse me, I have work to do.'

Miss Watts turned away from the desk and left the policeman there. Before she pushed her bulky frame through the swing-doors, Burrows called out:

'Thanks. And one last thing: would you

marry me?'

She didn't even turn around. Burrows shook his head, headed for the elevators.

The third-floor intensive-care rooms were all occupied. Burrows checked the board on the wall: only two lines didn't carry any names – Rooms 6 and 15. No one was at the desk so he walked down the corridor. Through the glass panel of the door, the little boy in Room 6 seemed asleep. Both his legs were trapped in casts, raised up. His head was all wrapped up, but judging by his size he didn't seem to be older than six or seven. Burrows pushed on until he got to Room 15. Inside, a nurse was checking something on the drip feed connected to the arm of the young woman lying on the bed. She turned as he pushed open the door.

'I'm sorry, sir; visitors are not allowed here.'

Burrows smiled at the young nurse, drew his badge out of his coat pocket.

'Police. Burrows. I've come to check on your patient. The hospital filed a report with us.' He glanced at the bed; very little of the body was actually visible. 'How's she doing?' he asked.

The nurse was pretty enough, with honest eyes, blond hair neatly tucked under her white hat.

'She's stable but still very weak.'

Burrows was used to seeing damaged

human beings, it was part of his job. Twenty-five years spent visiting crime scenes had made him immune to any emotional response, but he found himself gazing at the woman on the hospital bed, wondering how come she was here and not in the morgue. Her whole head was bandaged, leaving only the closed eyes exposed above the respirator. From the shoulders down, drip lines, casts and wires held the slender frame together. On the monitor, the green line showed a slight peak at regular intervals, witness to a struggling but still ticking heart.

'What happened to her?' he asked.

'Gunshot wounds, fractures, multiple contusions.' The nurse's voice sounded dispassionate and professional. 'If you'll follow me, I'll take you to Dr Willard – he'll be able to tell you more.'

They left the room. The nurse led the way to the end of the corridor, to a small office where a tall, greying man was busy entering data into a laptop computer. He looked up only when the nurse called to him.

'Doctor, this is Detective...' The nurse turned to the policeman, smiling apologetically.

'Burrows, Louis Burrows,' he filled in.

'He's here for the young woman in Fifteen.'

The surgeon stood up.

'Ray Willard. Nice to meet you.'

'Likewise.'

Burrows shook the outstretched hand, sat in the chair Willard was pointing to, next to him. The nurse slipped away quietly.

'So, Detective, what's the story?'

'Well, I wish I knew. We found absolutely nothing on that woman. No one has reported her missing and we've been unable to get an ID.'

Willard was sitting back in the chair. He said:

'Someone took the trouble of burning her fingertips, with acid apparently. Very thoughtful.'

Burrows frowned.

'Strange, real strange. No papers, no prints, nothing; some people went out of their way to make sure her body remained anonymous.'

'The plan didn't quite work out. She's still alive,' Willard remarked.

'Right, but she's not talking.'

Dr Willard shook his head.

'The last bullet we took out was close to the brain, too close. It's too early to tell but she might have suffered some damage to her vital functions.'

'She was found on the East Side, right?'

'That's what I heard. What do you think happened to her?'

'It's hard to tell.' Burrows shrugged. 'It could be drugs, or just jealousy. Who knows? Puerto Ricans are quick to kill.'

'You think she's Puerto Rican?'

'Well, she was picked up on their turf, and she does look like one of them.'

'Any leads down there?'

Burrows blew some air between his lips.

'That area is like the Wild West; they happily slaughter each other for the slightest problem, but as soon as they see a cop, suddenly no one speaks English. And those who do act like they don't know what you're talking about.'

Willard brushed his hair back with one hand.

'So, what now?'

'We just wait. When d'you think she might eventually wake up?'

'It's hard to tell. We've done all we can medically. Now it's out of our hands.'

That was exactly the way Burrows felt about the morning: it was out of his hands. He sighed. This was the kind of case he could have done without.

'What d'you mean, "still alive"?'

'It means that she's breathing, as in "not dead".'

Sal's dark gaze was fixed on Tommy's face. Apparently the news was quite a shock to the man. He just stood there, across the table from Sal, who still had his napkin tucked under his chin to avoid spilling tomato sauce on his expensive silk tie. Under his polo-neck sweater, Tommy was suddenly feeling hot. A botched job was bad news at the best of times, but to mess up on this particular contract was suicide, he knew that much. Sal's eyebrows were knitted tightly, a bad sign.

'But she took seven shots, two in the head! We even dropped her from a bridge, just to make sure! She's got to be dead...'

'You want to go to the hospital and check, Tommy?'

Sal's question was voiced too nicely – it made Tommy's stomach tighten even more. That was crazy. Paulie the driver was there, he had seen the hit, he knew the girl was dead. How could this be possible? Tommy shook his head, feeling like breeze was blowing freely between his two ears.

'I don't know what to say, Sal. I do good work, you know that. I pumped the girl full of slugs to make it look like it was niggers who done it. I ... I don't understand.'

Sal pulled out the napkin and dropped it on the table. Somehow he didn't feel hungry any more. This type of mistake was the worst thing that could happen to a man like him. The boss trusted him and he had never failed to repay that trust. But in times like this, even his unblemished record of thirty-plus years wouldn't be enough to clear him of blame.

'It's not good, Tommy,' Sal said, sounding like he was announcing doomsday.

Tommy was well aware it was not good.

'Look, Sal, even if she's still alive she's in bad shape. She hasn't talked...' he said, trying to sound sure.

Sal was looking at something on the wall behind the hitman, maybe one of the boxing photos hanging there, while slowly scratching his close-shaven left cheek with the back of his nails, upward. That was what Sal did when he concentrated on a problem, and it always made Tommy uneasy.

'She hasn't talked ... yet. She's in intensive care in the hospital,' he let out finally.

It was at times like these that the network of informants the family maintained all over town proved invaluable.

'I'll go and take care of it. Don't worry,' Tommy said quickly.

Sal had picked a cigarette from a pack in his jacket pocket. He took time to light it, blow out a small smoke cumulus towards the ceiling.

'Don't worry...?' he repeated, sounding like he found it almost funny. 'That was an easy job, Tommy, probably the easiest job you ever had. So when something that simple goes wrong, I get ... concerned, you know what I mean?'

The eyes were dead centre on Tommy's face.

'Sure, Sal...' Tommy had never been good with words, but today there was just no excuse he could possibly find to explain his failure. 'I'll go and finish the job,' he said, adding quickly, as if to reassure himself as much as Sal: 'I always do, right? You can count on me.'

Sal nodded. The left corner of his mouth lifted up slightly, but it couldn't be called a smile.

'I know I can, Tommy.'

Wednesday

The five closed-circuit television screens lined up facing the desk allowed for full monitoring of inside and around the club. The front entrance, the back street, the lobby, the dance-floor and the private 'VIP' room were all under constant surveillance from the office. Two men were assigned to this duty alone, and everything was recorded; that was the way Early wanted it. Altogether, with the dozen men he had moving around the place and the two outside security teams manning both ends of the road, he felt almost secure against any kind of surprise. Early was anything but careless. In a town as wild as Miami, especially around this neighbourhood, you had to suspect everyone and everything if you planned on living to retirement age. In the three years since he had opened his club, Drop Zone, Early had never been caught unawares, and that was proof enough that he was doing things the right way. By nature, he was constantly watching over his shoulder anyway, a disposition acquired at a young age. 'Wise man sleep with one eye open,' he always heard his father say as a child. That saying had kept Early watchful and alive.

Right now, he was sipping the last half of a tall rum and lime, squinting at screen number one. The buzzer sounded. Denton was on the other side of the door. Early signalled Mack to let him in and got back to the screen. Down there at the front, he could see Backalick and his team keeping the visitors in check. Until Denton got back to him with clearance, Backalick was going to stall and keep them waiting. It didn't matter that he knew who they were, that Early was in business with them and that relations between them were cool. Until he had clear instructions, no one was getting past Backalick. All the same, bulky and mean as he was, he was showing the visitors no disrespect. These guys were as vicious and crazy as he and his team were. Both sides knew that and this kept things levelled.

Denton came to the desk, waited until Early took his eyes off the screen.

'About a half a dozen ah dem down there. Another carful park up the road. Looks like him wan' flex.'

Early nodded slowly.

'Bring them to the private room ... Enrique and two men only.'

'What about them tools?'

'That all right. I meet yuh down there.'

Denton turned and walked out of the office. Early remained still for a minute or so, eyes on the screen but not really watching it any more. He had been expecting this visit for a few days. Still nothing from up north and, for once, no news was not good news. He would need to buy himself some time, but the situation had to be sorted out pretty fast, he knew that much. Early glanced at the drawer to his right but didn't go for it: this was his place, he was in no danger between these walls. Besides, this was a business call. He got up and simply glanced at Booker, the bulky shaven-headed man standing on the other side of the bank of screens; the man followed him out.

The corridor had been built to allow movements from the upstairs office to the lobby to be made without being seen from the dance-floor. It looked like a tunnel but carpeted and lit by coloured neon tubes. Only Early and his two most trusted ever used it. Right after the bend running around the rest rooms, a locked door led to the back entrance, just in case a quick and discreet exit from the club was required. Into the lobby were admitted only the select few on real close terms with Early, local or visiting celebrities of the show business, movie or modelling worlds. Somehow there were always more women than men in this part of the club. Some activities could take place there which were officially prohibited in the Drop Zone. Answering a few greetings, Early progressed through the lobby, shadowed by Booker. His face was, at the best of times, inexpressive. It was an asset in the kind of business he was in, especially for someone as young as him. Yet it was also true to the kind of person he was; calm, unemotional to the point of seeming cold to outsiders. But Early was a consummate actor also, and when he entered the private room an easy smile was set across his handsome face.

'Enrique, my main man! What's up, home?'

In the red leather couch, across the tastily decorated room, sat Enrique Sandoval. Tall and slim, with jet-black hair neatly slicked back, Enrique returned the smile but didn't get up.

'Hey, Early, how you doing?'

Of the two men with Enrique, only one was known to Early. Plump and bearded, his colourful shirt opened on a powerful torso, Carlos sat in an armchair to Enrique's right. Though he always seemed to be half asleep, Early knew from experience that the man was deceptively fast with a sharp business brain. He had been right-hand man to Luis Gallego, Enrique's predecessor. Gallego had, unfortunately, got caught up in a family feud and had returned to Cali to work there. That was what Enrique had told Early on taking over. Rumours in down-town Miami's player circles had it that Luis was in fact feeding sharks somewhere at the bottom of the deep ocean. With his expensive light grey suit, and slightly Indio features, Enrique was about as trustworthy as a rattlesnake. The other guard, young and thick from iron-pumping, stood behind the couch, eyes as cold as steel marbles set on Early. He was probably one of Enrique's personal crew.

'Could be better. You all want a drink?'

Early sat down across from his Colombian guest, Booker standing behind him, impassive as ever.

Enrique declined. 'No, we not staying.'

Denton was leaning against the un-attended bar, apparently relaxed.

'So, I guess your boss is a little worried,' Early said.

Enrique smiled, showing a perfect set of teeth.

'Worried? No. My boss is never worried,

27

hombre, you know that. He lets me worry.'

'Yeah, you got a hard job, Enrique.' Early nodded. 'But he sends you to find out why I'm late, right?'

Might as well get right down to business, he decided. Early had never been one to beat around the bush too long.

'*Claro que si, hombre*. Everybody got somebody to pay, you know, even the boss.'

'*Verdad*,' Early agreed, showing he hadn't grown up in Miami without mastering the local lingua franca. He shook his head.

'I'll tell you the truth, Enrique; my people in New York called this morning to let me know they had a little … collecting problem. That's what caused the delay.' From Early's confident tone of voice, you'd have thought he was talking about a minor problem. He told Enrique: 'But you can reassure your boss; it's being sorted out right now. Everything is OK.'

Enrique's eyes were locked on Early's as he listened to the explanation. He repeated: 'Everything's OK.'

'Yeah, man, you soon get your due.'

'OK.' A reassured nod, then the question: 'How soon?'

'Time for my people up north to get things together and do the transfer … say, a week.' Early sounded easy.

'A week?' Enrique's eyebrows rose ever so slightly.

28

Early opened up his hands, like he was surprised but not offended in the least.

'You sound like you don't trust me, Enrique.'

The Colombian was about Early's age, and just as steeped in the ways of the volatile business they ran.

'No, man, it's not like that...' Enrique smiled but his eyes didn't follow suit. '...but you know how this business works: words gets around that someone's late, then someone else gets late. People could lose respect, you know?'

Early made a face, like he understood.

'I see your point, man. But your boss knows I always deliver on time, right? We do good business together for some time now. I'm sure he won't think I'm disrespecting him.' A pause, two gazes weighing one another. 'Seven days, that's all I'm asking, as a favour. OK?'

In Carlos's half-closed eyes was the answer, but Enrique was the mouth here.

'Sure, Early, that's no problem. I'll explain to the boss, he knows you're a man of honour ... just like your father.'

Early didn't really want to hear his father mentioned here, especially by a man like Enrique who had no business making the reference. But he let it go and smiled.

'I always keep my word, amigo.'

The last word, although spoken no

differently from the rest, told Enrique he shouldn't get too familiar with Early. Subtle use of terms and tones often carried heavy meaning in conversations between men like them.

'Well, I'd like to stay and enjoy the music but it's a busy night,' Enrique said, getting up and fixing his jacket. Carlos got up too.

'You're always welcome, home. I guess I'll see you soon, right?'

Early was up and smiling at his dear Colombian friend.

'*Seguro!* Next week.' Enrique nodded, making his way towards the door.

'OK ... *compadres, hasta luego.*'

Only Carlos acknowledged the goodbye, his eyes meeting Early's for a fraction of a second before he followed Enrique out of the room. Denton led the guests back through to the entrance. As the door closed behind them, Early's face got back to its customary blank expression. He didn't even look at Booker as he said:

'You call New York. Find out what the hell happen down there.'

'She's fairly stable, out of intensive care. We're still drip-feeding her, and she needs reconstructive surgery on her jaws and cheekbones. We took her off the respirator twenty-four hours ago and she's doing pretty well. Her eyes are open but she's not responding to anything. There's a specialist coming in later today to check her out.'

Ray Willard rubbed his eyes with one hand, the receiver stuck between jaw and shoulder. One-forty-five was a little late for the police to call but Detective Burrows sounded very serious on the line.

'The FBI? Eh, sure … OK, I'll be waiting.'

He put down the receiver and sighed. He'd almost fallen asleep in front of the computer screen. The treatise he was working on was almost finished, but the last few pages were proving the hardest to write. With two days left before the meeting of the committee, his head was refusing to go on sifting through the data he had spent six months collecting. Overworked, stressed, he was twelve days away from a well-earned and much-postponed vacation. And now some FBI agents were coming down in the middle of the night to visit one of his patients! Seemed like everything was conspiring to prevent him from finishing his paper. Ray Willard got up, stretched his long and weary frame, then left the office to visit the hot-drink dispenser at the end of the corridor.

Just about the time Willard was picking up another cup of black coffee, two floors above, a broad-shouldered man in a trench coat emerged from the elevators. The

31

hospital was real quiet here, not like the lobby downstairs, where a string of casualties were keeping the place teeming with nurses, paramedics and uniformed cops. Good thing there weren't that many guards on duty at this late hour – it had made it all the easier for Tommy to slip by unnoticed and get to the right level. Sal's informant had passed on the room number, so it was just a matter of going in, doing it and getting out. He had calculated that he shouldn't spend more than ten minutes max in the building.

Tommy found the rooms listing on the board and was heading for the right side of the corridor when he heard the squeaking of wheels heading his way from beyond the bend. Sharp hearing was essential in a job like his. He ducked behind the empty desk, waited. Women's voices, talking low, the sound of the wheels blending in. They stopped by the elevator.

Calmly, Tommy waited for the elevator doors to open and close before he stood up. His hand left his right pocket and he moved down the dimly lit corridor towards the room. He got there, made sure it was the number he was looking for, glanced through the glass, and pushed the door open. But for an emergency lamp at the top right-hand corner of the bed, the room was dark and empty. In fact – and this made Tommy frown – the bed was also empty. He froze for a second, looked around him, even went to the small bathroom cubicle, but saw no one. How was this possible? Quickly now, Tommy stepped out of the room and checked the number affixed to the panel one more time. He wasn't crazy; it was the right room, the number Sal had given him earlier on. What the hell was going on here? The info dated from the afternoon – they couldn't have moved the girl out that fast! Unless … she had a relapse…? Ideas were racing through Tommy's brain, while in his gut a sinking feeling was setting in. Confused as he was, he heard them only as they had already turned the corner, male voices and footsteps. He turned just in time to hear:

'Hey, you! Police! Stay where you are…'

Two silhouettes were already running his way. Tommy wasn't a runner, had never been, but right then he had two choices and the first one wasn't really a valid option. So he eased his finger off the trigger, his hand left his pocket, and he tried to make the most of the twenty yards he had on the men coming after him. The stairs exit was right at the end of the corridor. Tommy crashed through the metal door and bolted down the stairs with all the speed his 225 pounds would allow him. Two flights down, he re-entered a corridor and pushed on, angry, frustrated and sweating. He had to get back on to the street, and fast, before more cops got in and closed the exits.

'Careful! Keep her real still, Marylee, hold her on this side... Yeah, hold the blanket. Steady, man! Right, together now: lift! Easy, Brenda: watch the tube! All right... On the mattress now, slowly, yeah... Here you are, baby ... you safe now.'

Speaking in a low voice, Ice directed the transfer from the big linen trolley to the van as if he'd been working as a paramedic all his life. At this time of the night, the employee parking lot was quiet, but he kept an eye out for any incoming car or anyone coming out from the service entrance all the same.

'Try to hook up the drip somewhere above,' Brenda told Ice. 'I took two more bags, so she can get enough to keep her nice for a little while.'

The young woman handed Ice two thick liquid-filled plastic bags.

'How she doing?' Ice asked.

'She's still weak but if she made it this far, she be all right. Careful with the neck brace when you move her out, OK?'

'Yeah. I got my boys to help me down there. You still on shift?'

'I got a couple more hours to do. I'll come to the house later.'

'Right.'

'And drive real slow, Ice; she got to be kept very still.'

'I be careful, don't worry.'

Ice listened to Brenda's instructions. A qualified nurse of several years' experience, she knew all about intensive-care patients. Though it was never advisable to move them, this was an emergency, and her input had been invaluable for the clandestine operation.

It had been their good fortune that Lisa got brought to the borough hospital where she worked. Ice had relied on her to set up the daring kidnapping she and Marylee had just so brilliantly executed. In and out within fifteen minutes; that was a clean mission, perfectly fulfilled. Now Lisa was in safe hands, with her people.

'You two are bad!' Ice congratulated the two-girl team.

Although he had wondered at first whether he should send back-up with them, just in case, Marylee insisted that at this late hour a couple of heavy-looking black men might attract attention. Two black nurses wouldn't draw attention from anyone, on the other hand. And she had been right; they had handled the job just fine.

'Later.' Brenda left to get back to her station.

Ice locked up the back of the van and got

back to the driving seat. He manoeuvred the van out of the parking lot and nodded to the black man manning the gate. Nothing unusual in a nurse being picked up by her husband after her night shift...

'How she doing?'

From the front, Ice glanced back to the slender shape wrapped up in a blanket on the mattress.

'She's been hurt bad, Ice. They got her jaws wired too. I guess it'll take a little time before she gets better,' Marylee explained.

Ice nodded.

'Yeah, we got her now, she's gonna get better.'

He paused just long enough to light the last half of his blunt, the flame briefly showing his narrowed eyes scanning the late-night traffic ahead.

'Then I'll take care of the motherfuckers who done her like that.'

A little cloud rose up from the thick cigar, wafted out of the window as Ice pulled out his mobile and dialled Early's number in Miami.

The elder of the two FBI agents sat on a metal chair, catching his breath.

'I want the area closed off and combed. Find this guy!'

The other agent, with close-cropped hair, his tie still firmly in place despite the late hour, frowned as he put down the phone. He walked to the window, peered through the blinds for a couple of seconds, then turned and leaned against the window.

'You said this girl was just out of intensive care, still under drip, Doc... How the hell could she walk out in the middle of the night and no one see her?'

Willard had been on shift for close to sixteen hours, and were it not for these two goons and their crazy story he'd be in bed by now. From his chair, he shrugged and shook his head.

'I really have no idea, but I don't believe she left by herself, if you want my opinion.'

Bronski had caught his breath now and seemed deep in a reflection of his own.

'Something weird's going on here, Jack,' he let out finally.

His partner's name was John Carter, but he always called him Jack.

'Something weird – you goddamn right, something weird! Three months' surveillance on a known Mafia operator and all we got to show is a missing undercover narcotics agent and a vanishing half-dead witness!'

'Witness?' Willard asked.

'We think the girl witnessed a murder. Maybe she even knows a lot more than that,' Bronski explained to the surgeon, rubbing the back of his neck wearily.

'A hit-man in a hospital in the middle of the night usually means someone knows a story they don't want them to tell! This was no courtesy call,' Carter stated, cynical as always. Tall and well built, he seemed the only one of the three men in the medical office who had any energy left.

'Who exactly is this girl?' Willard asked after a few seconds' silence. 'Can you tell me or is it ... classified?'

The two FBI men looked at each other, then Bronski said:

'We don't know.' He sighed, leaned back in the chair, but the metal back offered no comfort.

'It's a complicated story... We've been staking this operation owned by one of the big families, you know, mob guys...'

Willard was listening. Somehow he was curious about the young woman whose life he had saved.

'We found out this place, a restaurant-club, is being attended by certain city officials. That kind of tickled our curiosity, you know what I mean?'

Willard nodded, interested. Bronski went on.

'The owner is the nephew of one of the big bosses, an old-timer, and he's getting a lot of connections in high places. So we started checking him out. Then we found out something else: a DEA team, narcotics guys, also staking out the place. Apparently the owner's got narcotics connections and one of their agents managed to infiltrate the scheme, posing as a buyer. So now there's two teams working on the case.'

'Very popular spot!' Carter commented wryly.

'Yeah, right. The night before last, one of the DEA guys called his people in emergency. Apparently, his partner went in and never came back out.'

'Vanished.' Carter made a face.

'Disappeared. He was cutting a deal that night – they had him wired and ready to get evidence on our target. He went in, hung around, then suddenly they lost him.'

Willard waited.

'The DEA team went in, as you can imagine, gatecrashed the place – flak jackets, infrareds, dogs, the whole nine. So much for undercover. Turned the place upside down: no trace of their guy.'

'No drugs either!' Carter pointed out, bitter.

'And the girl?' Willard asked.

'The girl? Well, the DEA said their agent was talking to her outside, then they went in together. After that, nothing. The line went dead, they lost him.'

'Intriguing,' Willard said.

'You understand why we wanted to talk to the girl.'

'She wasn't inside either when the DEA team went in. They searched the whole place, but she'd simply vanished,' Carter added.

'Disappeared also?' Willard asked, puzzled.

'Right. The next thing we know, a local detective from 6–7 answers the missing-suspect call and sends us here.' Carter paused, looking frustrated as he said: 'And now she's vanished again.'

It all sounded a little wild to Willard. All he ever saw were the victims of stories like these, and he had long ago lost all but a casual interest in the reasons why bleeding bodies ended up on his operating table. Yet this girl had sparked his curiosity, first because very few survived the kind of injuries she'd suffered. And now the murky intrigue he'd just heard from the FBI guys just didn't seem to fit with what he saw in her. But then people are not very often what they seem to be. He asked:

'So you think that guy you saw upstairs came to finish her off, right?'

'Well, he wasn't carrying any flowers!' Carter sneered. 'That means she does know something.'

'What's bugging me now is who the hell got her out of here,' Bronski said quietly, like he was talking to himself.

Thursday

March had never been that warm in New York but this year seemed even worse than usual. An aggressive gust of wind had caught Early's face as they left JFK, and the short fifty-yard walk between the lounge and the awaiting vehicle reminded him how alien this town was to him. Born and raised in Miami, he had never felt comfortable in the Big Apple, even in summer. And it wasn't just the weather; the vibe wasn't his style either. Too much rushing, too much tension, a rhythm of life that he could never get used to. But he had a good reason for being here, and right now, reclining in the back of Ice's customised Dodge van, he was focusing his mind on that only.

'I don't want to worry you, Early, but I should tell you before we get there, she's in a bad way.'

Sitting beside the driver, Booker was listening in silence, as usual. He didn't like New York either, hated cold weather, but would have moved to Alaska if Early had asked him too.

'You told me she was recovering…'

Ice nodded slowly, touched the short

41

stubble around his chin.

'Yeah, she's OK ... she's out of danger, the doctors did a good job. You know she took seven slugs.' Ice waited a little, like he was about to say something, then changed his mind at the last moment. 'Not many people survive that.'

Ice turned from the driving seat and found Early's eyes looking at him. They were family, first cousins, and had worked together for years now, Ice taking care of the family's interests in New York, his home turf.

'So, what're you saying?'

'I'm saying, the girl got hurt and ... she ain't the same like before.'

Early didn't ask for details but Ice could feel he had to tell him straight.

'Your sister's not walking, man,' he said, then added quickly, 'I'm not saying she won't walk again, we need to see a specialist... And she ain't talking either.'

The car, bullet- and soundproof, was silent for a while. Ice waited for a sign, some reaction from Early, who was just staring ahead.

'She's not talking,' He heard Early say softly, as if to himself.

'They wired up her jaws, 'cause of the slug she took...' Ice stopped, feeling uncomfortable, but it had to be done.

'I got a doctor to check her out yesterday.

They took that thing off, but she ain't talking … yet,' he pointed out, trying to sound
hopeful.

'You're saying she's, like … paralysed,
right?'

Early's eyes were on Ice again.

'She can't move, it looks like,' Ice admitted, 'but the doctor said it's too early to tell.
She could get better.'

Early didn't comment on that. It was hard
to tell how he felt. His face was inexpressive
most of the time, but Ice could tell something was seething inside. He wanted to give
him at least one positive thing to hang on to.

'She was left on the East Side, Puerto
Rican territory, but the man who run things
down there is a friend. He gave me a lead, I
got my people checking things out.'

Early just nodded slowly.

'Right,' he said, then asked: 'The money?'

Ice sighed.

'No trace. Lisa picked it up, she was due
to fly back out the next day… She was supposed to call me the next morning before
the flight but she didn't.'

'A robbery?'

Early's face was as closed as they come.
But Ice knew what he was thinking. He
shook his head.

'Nobody could know. Unless she talked to
someone…' Ice paused. 'But I can't see it.'

'But she got hit and the money's missing,'

Early pointed out, his tone cold.

'Yeah… Can't figure it out.'

The van was quiet for a while. Traffic was thick on both sides, taxis and private cars rushing to the airport, more leaving and in a hurry to get to their homes. Early asked:

'Who knows about the money run?'

'Apart from me, only Marylee.'

'None of your boys?'

Ice shook his head.

'No, man, I can't trust nobody that far. This is family business.'

He had been thinking hard about it too since finding out Lisa had been shot. Something was not right here. He said:

'Lisa can't talk right now, but when she gets better she'll tell us what happened.'

'When she gets better,' Early repeated.

Outside, a light rain had started dropping from the overcast sky.

The residence was only one of the large walled domains of the well heeled who had chosen to hide in the relative safety of Long Island. Once you passed the electronically controlled security system at the gate, the long driveway to the mansion was discreetly monitored from two small brick houses on either side. Inside were two men on guard duty around the clock, with enough hardware to stand a determined assault on the site. Although the time for that type of all-out conflict between the families was over, the owner was an old-timer, and slept better knowing things were as he liked them to be.

The car that stopped in front of the steps was expected. A middle-aged man in a dark suit came down to the door. He could have been a butler but for his eyes, still and watchful at the same time. He didn't open the car door, but waited and looked straight at the man who stepped out.

'Hey, Pete, how you doing?' Sal asked.

'The boss is waiting for you,' Pete replied politely, like he had never met Sal before.

He led the way inside the house, through the large alcove that led to a huge living room, with high ceilings and statues, on down a few steps until they got to a heavy-looking wooden door. Pete knocked. You would have thought his knuckles made a barely detectable sound on the panel but someone spoke from inside. Pete opened the door and moved out of the way to let Sal enter.

The desk at the far end of the small office was old wood, polished and empty but for a beautiful Chinese vase. The flowers in it spread a touch of rose and white in an otherwise sober room. But the armchair behind it was empty. His hair all grey going white, with buttoned-up blue shirt and cardigan, the man who sat by the window set his eyes on Sal and watched him until he was close. Behind the glasses, which he only used to read the paper spread astride his lap, Mr Scaffone's dark eyes stayed still as Sal leaned over the old man and kissed him on both cheeks.

'Good morning, Uncle. How you feeling today?' Sal said nicely.

Mr Scaffone made a face, as he slowly took off his glasses.

'Bene ... va bene, figlio mio.'

Sal knew the old man liked to hear him speak Italian, but he was Brooklyn born and bred and, although he understood it well, he rarely used the language of the old country. He pulled up a chair and sat with his uncle.

Mr Scaffone sighed and placed the glasses in his cardigan pocket, then carefully folded the paper and put it on the small table set between the chair and the window.

'You see those trees by the pond ... over there, behind the wooden cabin...' Mr Scaffone was pointing through the window to a clump of tall pines to the right. 'That's where I used to sit every morning, after breakfast, when we moved to this place, a long time ago...' A warm smile flashed across Mr Scaffone's line-marked face.

'Your grandfather, he bought the land from a Jewish banker ... that was back in the early forties, just before the war... There were no other Italian families in the neighbourhood at that time. Well, when we moved in, I was about twelve … your father, he was just about ten… We used to go and fish in the pond, then, if we catch a fish, we go down to that place near the cabin and make a fire, to fry the fish… Then we eat it.'

Mr Scaffone shook his head, his eyes on the park, through the window.

'Your grandmother, she was always afraid we drown in the water, you know… She used to tell us some mermaids lived in the water and they would eat us.'

The old man let out a brief chuckle as he recalled long-gone days of his childhood. His tone was softer, weary almost, as he said:

'Now the doctor tells me I can't go down there no more. It's too far for me to walk, he says.' Mr Scaffone sighed, taking Sal as a witness to his plight.

'I can't even walk around my own place, can you believe this?'

He stood up carefully, shrugging. Sal was up before him, offering a supportive arm.

'But he's a doctor. They study very hard to become doctors, so they know what they're talking about.'

Thin looking in his pressed slacks and grey cardigan, the old man motioned Sal towards the other side of the room where heavy leather armchairs surrounded a sculpted coffee table.

'So I don't go there no more.'

The stroke that had nearly taken Giuseppe Scaffone away two years before had left him able to perform only the most basic physical activities. Although he had made a better-than-average recovery, he was still under the close surveillance of his old-time physician and friend, Dr Rossini.

'*E come sta la famiglia, figlia mio? Bene?*' Old Giuseppe asked when they were comfortably seated.

'*Bene, molto bene*, Uncle.'

The old man nodded. He dearly loved Sal's two boys whom he had by the house almost every weekend, entertaining them with wild stories about his early days.

'You spend time with the family, Sal?'

'Yes, I'm home with them every day, Uncle.'

'That's good. A man must spend time with his children. That's the only thing that's important, the children. Don't forget this.'

Mr Scaffone nodded to emphasise the advice he was dispensing to his nephew.

'And how's business?' he asked.

'Good ... things working OK,' Sal answered soberly.

He knew full well that he had not been called in to talk about fishing and parental duties.

'Hmm... You know, the doctors don't want me to look after no business. They say I have to relax, take it easy...' Mr Scaffone paused before adding, 'That's why I was lucky to have you to take things over, Sal.'

It sounded like a compliment.

'Everything is running well, Uncle. We're turning over well … Benny comes down every week…'

'Yeah, I know. Benny tells me business is good… But I have to ask you, you know, just in case.'

Mr Scaffone stopped to pull a thin metal box out of his cardigan pocket. He opened it and took out a flat white tablet which he carefully placed on his tongue. While he closed the box and returned it to the pocket, Sal filled a glass from a tinted water jug on the table. The old man took a slow gulp and swallowed.

'Three a day. They help keep my blood pressure low, Dr Rossini says,' he told Sal. Then he came back to where he had left off, just as Sal knew he would.

'You know, Sal, in case you had any problems, things you don't want to talk about with Benny, you can always come to me, about anything. Sometimes I can still help. My body's getting older but my mind is still working good. Maybe you prefer to discuss certain things with me directly, you know, maybe…'

This way of saying 'maybe' had sometimes been misunderstood by people when Giuseppe Scaffone was running his affairs, in the old days. They had always found out later what he meant exactly. But Sal knew, so he said:

'Well, life is never perfect, you know, Uncle. I have a few things I'm working on, some small ... problems, you know, minor things... But I'm taking care of that, don't worry, it's not affecting the business.' Sal tried to sound sure of himself.

The years, the stroke, the heavy doses of medicines, nothing had altered the way Giuseppe Scaffone's eyes could focus and drill through a person at certain times.

'Everything affecting a man affects his business, *figlio mio*,' he said simply.

Sal was starting to feel very uneasy. Although he was trying to remain composed, something was dancing in the pit of his stomach, like an air bubble bouncing around. How much did the old man know already about his troubles? He decided to come clean – well, almost...

'I've had a few problems lately, it's true. The Feds, they been at my place, asking questions, snooping around. They say some city officials come to my restaurant, so they're investigating them, that kind of thing. I told them I can't help it if the guys love Italian food... And I have good relations with some of the city guys, nothing wrong with that. It's just some games they like to play, looking for bad apples in their top brass. You know how these guys are!'

Mr Scaffone was listening patiently.

'Yeah, I know.' He shook his head slightly. 'They have to try to shake us down from time to time ... I was a little worried. I thought it was the DEA or something like that...'

A pin shot down the air bubble; cold air froze the pit of Sal's stomach.

'DEA?' He forced a thin smile to his lips. 'I'm not their type of customer,' he said, then added, 'Some of them even come to eat down there with their wives. Their money is welcome too.'

Old Giuseppe sketched a little smile too.

'Better a good dog than a bad friend. At least you always know what the dog wants from you.'

Sal had never had the taste for his uncle's Sicilian proverbs or their English translations. Right then he wasn't too sure what this one meant and how it could apply to him. But he nodded.

'I'd rather keep these kinds of friends happy with a bottle of Scotch once in a while.'

'Good. Good,' was all that Mr Scaffone said.

But now Sal knew that he knew. And the old man knew that there was no need to ask any more questions; Sal had gone against his formal instructions and got involved in things that had now gotten out of hand. But if he felt angry about it his face didn't let it show. He cleared his throat, seemed to remember something, and told Sal:

'Go and look inside the top drawer in my desk. I found some old pictures of your father when he was a kid. You're gonna laugh.'

Only the eyes moved. They were focused on Early's face, searching, probing, sending silent messages. The brace was propping her head up, keeping her neck still. Lisa's hands, her long, slender fingers that used to fly so effortlessly over the ivory keys of a piano, just lay on the armrests of the wheelchair, lifeless. The tips were all black, darker than her brown skin.

Even after the first half-hour, Early was trying hard not to but couldn't help staring at his sister's tortured face. The bullet that had entered through her left cheek, from above, had crashed its way through the bone to the other side, leaving a dark spot the size of a quarter on her lower right jaw where it exited. The wound was still fresh and puffy, swelling the side of the young woman's mouth in a grotesque way. But however ugly it was, the wound wasn't fatal. The other head shot should have taken her life. The bullet was meant to drill right through her skull but, for some strange reason, it had stopped just short of her brain. The surgeons had had a hard time getting the slug out. Though her head was covered by a baseball cap, the beginnings of a dark scalpel line were visible just above Lisa's temple. Five more slugs had ripped through the woman's body, from a short distance, one of them lodging near her spine.

Early understood now why Ice had been so embarrassed talking about the state of Lisa. Strangely, though he was happy she wasn't dead, the damage to her face had hit him unexpectedly when he had walked in. He didn't show it, out of habit, but inside the pain jolted his guts like the slicing of a cold blade. To look at Lisa's disfigured features, where grace and beauty had been only a few days earlier, took a lot out of Early. And then his sister couldn't talk. He thought he had seen her eyes widen when he'd come in earlier, but her gaze was so still, so ... vacant, as she simply sat there and stared his way. Early had hugged his younger sister, held her tight, feeling emotionally aware in a way he hadn't felt since their father's death, two years earlier. Yet it was weird not to feel any response from Lisa, her body insensitive to his embrace, rigid almost.

'She can eat?' Early asked, his eyes still on Lisa's.

'The doctor took the wires out yesterday,

but her jaw still hurts. I get her to drink through a straw,' Marylee explained.

She'd known both Early and Lisa since she'd started out with Ice five years before.

'The doctor know why she can't move?' he asked.

'He says she gotta see a specialist.' As if to reassure Early somehow, Marylee added: 'I look after her, man, don't worry. She'll be all right.'

Early nodded slowly. He knew Marylee would do everything she could for Lisa. But Lisa was sitting there in front of him, paralysed, almost lifeless, like a shadow of the sister he had known. The girl whose songs had always been around couldn't talk any more; her dancing feet now sat motionless on the metal wheelchair footrests.

Early got up, walked through to the kitchen, where Ice was busying himself around the cooker. He went to the open bay windows, stepped on to the veranda, where climbers had eaten up the white wooden panel surrounding it. A gushing water fountain with an arrow-shooting angel was throned in the middle of the well-kept garden. Ice came outside, produced a long tobacco roll out of his jeans pocket.

'I kept that for you. It's straight out ah Yard.'

Early hesitated a second or two; he needed to be raw for the action, but then there was no target as yet. Above all, he had to smooth out the edges of the cold anger seething inside his guts. He took the blunt, lit it at Ice's offered lighter flame. The draw was smooth, light to the palate, yet with a peppermint-like twinge that lingered on the tongue.

'How the music business going?' he asked.

'Up and down. I got a good run from this ragga hip-hop track I told you about last time. I got a few good artists but some are hard to handle. It's a dog race, you know that.'

Early nodded. He knew how tough the life of a producer could be.

A white cloud was rising to meet the climbers. With his mind levelled out by the quality herbs, after the shock of seeing the extent of his younger sister's damage, Early was ready to deal with the matter.

'What you got?'

Ice made a face.

'Not much. We got her car back, it's in the garage. We searched it down, even dusted it for prints, but it's completely clean.'

Ice scratched his stubbled chin, the way he always did when puzzled by something, then added:

'It looks like a professional job.'

'The money?' Early's eyes squinted through the smoke. The veranda smelled like a corner of the bushy Jamaican green hills.

'Nothing.' Ice was shaking his head. He

took the blunt from Early, pulled twice on it. 'But we found something,' he said after blowing out.

Early waited, watched Ice's hand come out of his jeans back pocket. It was a white paper napkin, neatly folded in four. Early took it, spread it carefully on his left hand.

'Sciachitana,' he read, frowning.

'Sounds Italian,' Ice said, drawing on the blunt.

'Where you get that?'

'It was stuck in the corner of the back seat, pushed between the cushions.'

Early looked at Ice.

'The back seat,' he repeated. He brought the napkin to his nose, sniffed it lightly. His eyes narrowed, then he said:

'Lisa got asthma, she always carries a tissue on her, to wet it with medicine.'

'She must have pushed the napkin there, like she knew she was gonna get hit,' Ice reflected.

Early inhaled, kept silent for a few seconds, his eyes beyond the garden gate.

'Lisa's a soldier,' he said quietly. Then he turned to Ice.

'You said there was no prints...'

'We dusted the door handles, the wheel, the gearshift handle ... Nothing.'

Early's eyes came back to the white napkin with the foreign name in red and green letters.

'I think you're right, Ice: it's a professional job.' He nodded slowly.

It was late and the last couple of diners had just gone through the door. But at the last table, near the entrance to the kitchen, the fat man in his braces and rolled-up sleeves just kept swallowing big lumps of spaghetti. From the bar where he sat, Tommy watched him carefully rolling the long reddish threads around his fork, lifting it up to his mouth, then leaning back and letting it all slide down. It was like watching a baby hippopotamus gulp down food at the zoo. The hair on the man's head was sparse, his eyes small and deep set into the sockets. Where he had loosened his tie, you could see podgy rose flesh and a thin gold chain. Had Rafaele Moscelli been taller, he could have looked dangerous. But with his barrel chest, flabby waist and oversize behind, he resembled a chubby baby, and walked like one. That's why everyone called him Bambino – behind his back, of course. But looks can be very deceiving, especially in Bambino's case. He had been Don Scaffone's most efficient and trusted executioner for twenty-five years, and inspired a holy fear in everyone who knew who he really was.

Young Rafaele was only a child when both his parents were murdered in the old country. He was spared because the killers missed the terrified little boy hidden inside the clothes chest where his mother just had time to slip him. Don Scaffone, a distant cousin of his and a few years older, had sent for him from New York where he had recently settled. This was many years before, but Rafaele had never forgotten he owed him his life. He was a simple boy, not too bright but devoted, content just to do his cousin's bidding without question.

Though he wasn't intelligent in the usual sense of the term, Don Scaffone had found out that the chubby country boy had a very special skill: he could kill inventively. When Bambino was sent after someone, the Don could be certain of two things: the target was never missed and the police would never find out who did it. Bambino specialised in fake accidents; car crashes, electrocutions, drug overdoses, fatal falls... His greatest pleasure in life was to report to Don Scaffone and see him smile and say to him in his quiet way: 'Good work, Rafe, good work.'

Bambino had finally eaten his fill and was sitting back, sipping a little wine like a gourmet on a night out. He had arrived a few hours earlier and quietly taken the last table at the back. His unexpected arrival had considerably darkened Sal's already sombre mood. These last few weeks had not been rosy for him. The police incident had forced him to play heavy handed. The body of the undercover DEA agent had not been found, and was unlikely to be, but then there was this business of the girl which still bugged him. And all because that clumsy fool Tommy had botched up a job for the first time in his sinister career! Sal didn't believe in bad luck as such, but he couldn't help but feel everything had been against him lately.

Sal came out of the kitchen, where he had been talking to his cook. He winced when he saw that Bambino was still there, his bulging stomach full now, slowly finishing his wine.

'How was the food, Rafaele?' Sal smiled at the fat man. Like he really cared whether he'd enjoyed his meal.

'Bene, molto bene.'

Bambino hardly ever expressed anything, be it pleasure or pain. He had once suffered a deep gash to his forehead on a job, the only time he had almost failed to complete a contract. For all his face showed while the doctor was sewing him up, he could have been eating an ice cream.

'Good, good.' Sal nodded.

He went to the bar, exchanged a frustrated look with Tommy, still sitting there, and poured himself a tall glass of grappa. Finally Bambino got up, slowly, rolled down his sleeves, adjusted his tie with great care, then

59

put his jacket and coat back on and started crossing the room towards the door.

'*Grazie, Sale, arrivederci.*'

He barely glanced Sal's way while talking, as if moving on took all his concentration. Yet the couple of seconds during which their eyes met sent a cold feeling down Sal's stomach. Bambino had always made him feel uncomfortable; he couldn't help it. It was like the man wasn't really human or something.

'OK, Rafe, see you later.'

Sal and Tommy watched the short fat man open the restaurant door and disappear into the night.

'Sonofabitch!' Sal let out with disgust. He was impeccably dressed as always, in a light grey suit and blue tie, but his eyes looked tired and his face drawn.

'Take it easy, Sal; just because the guy came in to eat doesn't mean nothing.'

From behind the bar, where he was switching to whisky, Sal threw Tommy a look of pure contempt.

'What are you: fucking stupid?' he exploded. 'That fat bastard ain't come in here for two years. Last time he did, Louie the Fizz was eating in with his buddies from Philly and a bunch of broads. You remember how they found Louie two days later?'

Tommy didn't answer but frowned as he recalled the occasion. The hotel room when the police burst in looked like the set of a horror movie. Two dead Latina girls, one stabbed in the throat, one with two bullets in her chest and a butcher's knife in her hand. And Louie the Fizz, naked on the bed, his dick cut off and clutching an automatic.

'I'm gonna hit that fat chump first, that's what I'm gonna do!' Sal was standing by the bottle rack, the wall mirror reflecting the wicked glint in his eyes.

'Sal, please don't go *pazzo!* You can't hit Bambino...'

Tommy just about managed to move out of the way as the splinters of Sal's glass flew past him after it shattered against the bar.

'You fucking goon! I can hit whoever I want. I'll do it myself this time, and then I'll pop you too, like I should have done in the first place!'

Sal sounded really out of his head now. The half-bottle of whisky and several glasses of wine he had gone through since earlier in the evening had only helped to raise his level of frustration.

'I wouldn't be in this mess if you had done your fucking job properly. Call yourself a hit-man! You couldn't even take care of a girl! Now that molyan bitch is somewhere in New York City waiting for the right time to grass my ass. D'you know what's gonna happen if the cops find her before we do?'

Sal let his fury settle on the question. Tommy had no illusions about what would happen. He was the one who had hit the undercover cop and the girl. The former would tell no tale, but the latter was still alive and able to send him down. Now it didn't matter much that Sal gave the orders; Tommy's ass was first in line. That much was clear to him.

Friday

Miss Watts wasn't in a particularly good mood this morning. She didn't know why exactly, but it felt like one of those days when somehow, as soon as your feet got off the bed and touched the floor, you knew it was not going to be a good day. Yet she cooked herself breakfast, put on the red-and-black dress her sister had sent her from England, and took time to play her favourite Shirley Bassey song before she left her Bed Stuy apartment. But as soon as she hit the street, the greyish sky finally decided to open up and free its awaiting raindrops on to her permed hair, and that ruined any chance of a pleasant day.

Sure enough, she had hardly settled down behind her desk when trouble started in the form of an old grey smelly hobo with a gaping head gash and a shaggy black dog he wouldn't be separated from. She tried, not very diplomatically it must be said, to get the man to leave his furry companion outside. But the tramp said no; the dog's name was Herbie, and he had to stay with him at all times. Said Herbie was his army buddy and they did everything together. Sensing she was about to lose her temper with the man, Miss Watts called two orderlies, who patiently tried to explain to the hobo, whose name was Albert, that basic hygiene, common sense and respect for the New York City Health Board regulations made it impossible for Herbie to accompany him inside. They would tend to his wound quickly while the dog waited outside and the two of them would then be reunited after the briefest delay.

But Albert, stubborn as a donkey, refused point blank to see their point and said he had never in the past ten years been separated from Herbie and that was that. The two orderlies, who were starting to lose patience with Albert, and also had problems with his very unpleasant smell, then explained that he would have to either leave the dog outside or leave the hospital with his bleeding head. That got Albert mad. He sprung up, took the rest of the waiting crowd, patients, nurses, doctors and cleaning staff as witnesses, and started berating a society in which a man like him, who had bravely fought for his country and shed his blood in two wars, was refused healthcare in New York City, capital of the free world.

And sure enough, as with anything relating to freedom and human rights anywhere in the USA, and especially in New York, the old veteran's slurred but impassioned speech touched the sensibilities of the assembled crowd. Whereas most had, up to then, watched the stand-off with amusement, they now began to loudly debate the issue of whether Albert wasn't in fact being denied his rights. Sensing he was now in a strong position to drive home his point, Albert then started chanting, in an unbearably loud and broken voice, 'The Star-Spangled Banner.' Herbie the shaggy dog had watched the whole thing with total indifference, but on hearing his master's chant he started barking in time with the song. Within minutes, the entry hall of the hospital looked like a student campus on a hot, rebellious day. Behind her desk, where she had wisely retreated, Miss Watts took off her glasses and started to cry.

It was this surrealistic scene that greeted Marylee as she entered the hospital foyer. She took one look around the place, didn't quite understand what was taking place but realised right away that the chaos was all to her advantage. So she strolled to the lifts, found one waiting and rode up to the third floor. The young white woman behind the desk looked up from her magazine, smiling.

'Good morning.' Marylee smiled back, not quite sure how she was going to play her hand.

'Good morning,' the nurse said.

'I'm looking for my cousin. I was told she was brought here a few days ago. She was shot. I've just found out and I'd like to see her.'

Petite, pretty, with a baby face and large innocent eyes, Marylee could make anyone believe anything. But her cute looks and helpless ways concealed a very sharp mind and a fearless disposition.

'Oh, the young woman with the head wounds, yes... She's your relative?'

'Yeah, she's my first cousin. We didn't know what happened to her, we've been looking all over for her. The police told me someone was brought in who fitted her description.'

'We didn't know who she was, she was really badly hurt, but the doctors saved her.'

'Thank God!' Marylee's eyes were all soft, her hands clasped together. 'Could I see her, please?'

The young nurse's face dropped a little.

'I really don't know how to tell you this,

miss, but ... your cousin disappeared.'

'Disappeared?' Marylee repeated, frowning.

The nurse seemed embarrassed.

'Two days ago. She was just out of intensive care. I tended to her early in the evening, but when I went back to check on her later that night she was gone. I ... we just don't know what happened.'

Marylee seemed dumbstruck.

'Gone? But ... how? You said she was badly hurt! How could she walk out, and nobody see her leave?'

The poor nurse would have liked to have been able to offer a valid explanation, but there was none, so she just shook her head sadly.

'I ... I don't know ... I'm sorry.'

'Oh my God!' Marylee wailed. 'Have mercy...' She was holding on to the desk.

'Would you like to sit down?' The nurse had come over and placed a sympathetic hand on Marylee's shoulder.

'I'm all right...'

'I don't know what to say, I know it must be horrible for you.' The young nurse was trying her best to find the right words.

'Could I see the doctor who saved her? Is it possible? I'd really like to meet him...' The flutter in Marylee's voice was so real the nurse was glad she could do something to help.

'Sure, I think he's still on shift. Come along, we'll go and find him.'

The two women walked down the corridor, the nurse leading and gently holding Marylee's arm as she so often did for patients, day in, day out. They got to the last room on the corridor, where a man was on the phone with his back to the door. The nurse waited, knocked lightly on the panel when he put down the receiver.

'Dr Willard, this young lady would like to see you. She's a relative of the young woman from Room Fifteen, the one who ... disappeared.'

She said the word like she was ashamed. Marylee looked at the doctor with his white overalls and greyish hair. His eyes met hers and he got up, stretched his hand to her.

'Hi, I'm Ray Willard. Come in, please.'

'Denise Watson.' Marylee shook the offered hand. 'I was coming to see my cousin, but the nurse said she...'

'I was explaining to Miss Watson...' The young nurse sounded embarrassed, as if it was all her fault somehow.

'That's all right, I'll talk to Miss Watson. Thank you, Sharon.'

The nurse left.

'Please, have a seat.' Dr Willard quickly moved a pile of folders from a plastic chair, moved it towards his visitor.

'The nurse said you saved my cousin's

life,' Marylee started. 'I want to thank you for this.'

'She was in pretty bad shape but we managed to make her a little better,' the doctor replied modestly.

'But she wasn't well enough to walk out of here.'

A perplexed look crossed Dr Willard's face. He paused before speaking.

'Your cousin is paralysed from the neck down, Miss Watson.'

There were several silent seconds, Marylee's eyes searching the doctor's.

'Paralysed...?'

'She's been hurt very bad. It's almost a miracle she made it.'

Marylee closed her eyes briefly, bit her bottom lip. Sighing deeply, she asked:

'Are you saying she'll never walk again?'

Dr Willard rubbed the back of his neck with one hand.

'We took seven bullets out of your cousin's body, one from her skull and one from her back, very near the spine. Medically speaking, her nervous system isn't damaged but she cannot move. We were waiting for her to get a little stronger before running more tests but...'

'So she might get better?'

'Well, apart from the gunshot wounds, your cousin suffered broken bones and severe contusions... She also went through a psychological shock, as you must understand.'

Marylee's gaze was fixed on the surgeon's eyes, probing. He could only be honest about it.

'It's still too early to tell whether her paralysis is physiological or psychosomatic.'

Realising the young woman might not understand fully what he meant, the doctor added:

'What I mean is that she could be permanently paralysed, although we haven't identified actual reasons for this, or her nervous system could simply be in shock. It happens when someone gets hurt as bad as that.'

'So she could get better, maybe?' Marylee asked again.

The slightest word of hope from a doctor always sounds like a promise to most people. Dr Willard knew this only too well. He said:

'Maybe. She needs time. And specialist care.'

Marylee nodded, looking deep in concentration.

'Do you know what happened to your cousin, Miss...'

'Watson. Call me Denise.' Marylee shook her head. 'I don't know. She just went missing last Sunday.'

'How did you find out she was here?'

A logical question.

'The guys at the precinct said someone was brought in with gunshot wounds. She fitted the description so I came over.'

'What's your cousin's name?'

'Jessie.'

'Jessie...' Dr Willard repeated. 'Tell me, Denise, why would someone want to harm your cousin?'

'I don't know,' Marylee answered, feeling the intensity of the surgeon's light-coloured eyes on hers. To escape them, she glanced around the room, at the medical volumes and cardboard boxes of files filling the metallic shelves.

Dr Willard sighed, shook his head.

'Whatever it is, some people must want her dead pretty bad,' he said in his soft voice.

'Why d'you say that?'

'The same night she disappeared a man was on the ward looking for her. It wasn't anyone from your family...!'

If there was any humour in the doctor's remark, it wasn't intended.

'Did you see him?' Marylee asked.

'No, but the FBI guys did. He managed to lose them.'

'FBI?' Marylee repeated.

Dr Willard made a face.

'According to them, your cousin Jessie might be involved with some very dangerous people. They think she has certain information on them, they want her because of that.'

Then he said:

'Strictly speaking, I'm not supposed to tell you this.'

Marylee said nothing for a few seconds, the relative silence of the hospital's upper floor floating around the little office.

'Look, Doc, I don't know what happened, but Jessie hasn't done anything wrong, I know that. She's innocent.'

'She looks that way,' Dr Willard said quietly.

They said nothing for a while, Marylee looking lost in thoughts of her own, the surgeon silently observing the young woman sitting across from him. Then he said:

'You don't seem worried about her whereabouts.'

Marylee looked up at him, bore his gaze and replied quietly:

'She's safe…'

The man just nodded, said nothing. Then Marylee added:

'But, like you said, she needs specialist help.'

'And that's why you came here today…'

'You saved her life. Who else could I go to?'

It was so simple, so logical… A tired smile lit up the seasoned surgeon's features.

'You're a brave young woman, and you love your cousin very much, I can feel that.'

'She didn't deserve to die like that, that's why God protected her,' Marylee said.

'He shall give his angels charge over thee, to guard thee in all thy ways,' Dr Willard recited.

The office didn't look much like a church but right there and then Marylee felt something go through her body, like a fragrant, soothing breeze borne by the doctor's words.

He saw the intrigued look on the young woman's face, smiled at her.

'My hands learned skills to allow me to save lives, but in the end it's always down to Him.'

Marylee nodded, thought about this, then said:

'Her name is Lisa, and with your help I know she'll get better.'

Dr Willard waited a moment before asking:

'How do you know you can trust me?'

'God trusts you every day with people's lives, doesn't He?'

Dr Willard seemed impressed by the young woman's wisdom. He nodded.

'I guess He does.'

Sighing, he stretched to get hold of the phone on his desk.

'Who you calling?' Marylee asked.

He looked her straight in the eyes before dialling.

'I've got to call a colleague to finish my shift for me. You're going to ask me to come with you, aren't you?...'

Outside, a timid New York spring sun lit up the street while the still-crisp air pricked the faces of passers-by. But inside the weathered office smelling of cold coffee and cologne, it was as warm and stormy as a Louisiana summer.

'Am I under arrest?'

'No, sir, you're just helping us with our enquiries.'

'Look, guys: I think I've helped you enough. You come and take me from my house while I'm having breakfast with my wife and kids, you ask me all these questions over and over again ... I told you all I know. Now I'm out of here, OK? If you want to stop me, then you charge me ... if you got anything on me.'

Sal was fast losing patience with the FBI agents' polite but persistent ways.

'One last question, sir, if you don't mind.' From the sound of his voice, you would have thought Bronski was a travel agent selling a plane ticket. 'On the evening in question, do you recall a customer dressed in a dark blue suit, around Six-two, a hundred and eighty pounds, tanned skin, wearing tinted glasses?'

'How many times you gonna ask me that? I told you, I don't remember anybody. I see hundreds of guys like that every week, I run a busy place. I never seen the guy you're talking about. Maybe he was there, I don't know.'

'He was there OK! We know he was inside your place, and we know he never came out. That's not a maybe, that's a fact. So we have good reasons to think something happened to him inside and that you know about it. It's time you stopped bullshitting us and started talking, all right?'

Carter had left the far desk near the window and walked right up to Sal's chair, stopping a few inches from his face. A clean college boy with a traditional Midwest up-bringing, he had no love for the smartass, slick-dressing, wiseguy type Sal represented. Calmly, Bronski called out:

'Easy, Jack, easy. Let's keep this clean.'

Disgusted, Carter quit staring into Sal's eyes and went back to look at the traffic below the window.

'What's the matter with this guy?' Sal said.

'Jack knew the DEA agent we're talking about. You understand he's taking this a little personal ... OK, Sal, what about the girl? What happened to her?'

'Look, you ask me already and I told you: I don't know what girl you're talking about,

OK. Hundreds of girls pass through my place every week. How am I gonna remember every one of them?'

Bronski didn't like Sal's kind any more than Jack did. Born of Polish parents, he had little love for Italians, but in his thirty years with the Bureau he had learned to put his personal feelings aside in his work. Patiently, he explained:

'Sal, the reason we're so interested in this young woman is that she was talking with the DEA agent when we lost contact. She must know what happened to him, that's why we want to find her. The fact that she disappeared also makes us all the more suspicious, I'm sure you can understand that.'

It was getting harder for Sal to play dumb, so he just shrugged.

'Sure, I understand that, but it's nothing to do with me. Maybe some of my guys are playing games I don't know about...'

Carter turned away from the window just long enough to throw a really dirty look at the man in the chair. Bronski simply nodded with a blank stare.

'Look, this is a really weird story, I know that. I'll check around, and if I find out anything, I'll let you know. Can I go now?'

There were a few empty seconds before Bronski said:

'Sure, you're free to leave.'

Sal got up, straightened his tie out of habit, adjusted his expensive overcoat.

'OK, you guys, have a nice day. See you around.'

He was already opening the door when Carter said:

'Yeah, you will.'

'I was getting worried,' Paulie said as Sal got into the Lincoln.

'These fucking guys!' Sal smirked.

'Where we going?' Paulie asked as he sharply slipped the car into the busy downtown traffic, gesturing to a driver who blew his horn at him. Short and wiry, with a ferret-like face, Brooklyn born and bred, Paulie was the nervous type.

'Take me home. I'm starving. These goons came in on me right in the middle of breakfast. Then you go to the restaurant and wait for Tommy.'

'What the Feds want with you?' Paulie asked.

'Ah, same thing as the other night. They're still looking for their DEA buddy.'

'He's gonna be missing a long time,' the driver said without humour. Even when he made a joke, Paulie hardly managed a smile.

'They're looking for the girl too,' Sal remarked sombrely.

Paulie knew better than to make any smart remark about that. Although he wasn't

76

directly at fault, he had been on the hit with Tommy, and he knew the blunder was making Sal really sore.

'Tommy's got guys checking out for her,' he said, keeping his eyes on the road.

'She could be halfway to Puerto Rico by now! If Tommy had done his job, I wouldn't have to worry about that no more. If the Feds find her before us, it's all over for me.'

Paulie thought about this for a moment, then he said:

'You know, Sal, I think maybe she's hiding from the cops too.'

Sal didn't answer right away. He glanced at Paulie, reflected on the idea for a while.

'You could be right...'

'She didn't walk out of the hospital all by herself,' Paulie added, sensing that his way of thinking pleased the boss.

'Right. You're a smart guy, Paulie, you know that?' The compliment went straight to Paulie's brain. He almost smiled. He added:

'Anyway, if the cops find her, we'll know about it. Our friends won't let her get to court... Right, boss?'

This time, Sal turned to his driver and patted him on the back of the head.

'Right, Paulie. You know, you're getting smarter all the time.'

Paulie didn't answer. He had always thought he could get a better job than just being a driver. He was feeling like this might turn out to be a very good day.

'You trust that white man 'cause he's a doctor?'

Ice's question wasn't answered right away. Marylee had been with him long enough to know his views on trust. She glanced at Early, who seemed to be absorbed in the Brooklyn street scenes outside.

'I trust him 'cause he cares whether Lisa walks again or not... And he's a man who works with God.'

'What?'

From behind the wheel of his van, Ice sounded like he thought his wife had suddenly lost her mind.

'He saves lives and he prays, all right? And I feel he's gonna make a difference for Lisa, that's why I believe he's not gonna give her up to the cops.'

'What if you're wrong?' Ice asked.

'I'm not wrong,' Marylee replied firmly. 'What has he got to gain from giving her up?'

No one spoke for a while. Early was thinking about it, but he was keeping his opinion to himself. He had not talked to the tall white doctor with the soft eyes, keeping himself out of sight, leaving Ice to deal with the man.

'I guess we got no one else to turn to

anyway,' Ice conceded after while.

He didn't think Marylee should be made aware that Early had asked him to find out Dr Willard's address. Maybe he'd tell her later.

Dr Willard had seemed happy to see Lisa again, checked her blood pressure, her eyes, felt her neck and limbs. He said she was getting better, but then again doctors usually declare their patients are, unless their condition shows obvious signs of deterioration. All the time, while the doctor was examining her wounds, Lisa kept still, her face almost peaceful despite the disfigurement.

'The man said she'll walk again?' Early asked, breaking his silence.

'He said it's too early to tell. He thinks she might be in some kind of shock, like her nervous system seized up or something.'

Marylee looked at Early, sitting silently across from her in the back of the van. She knew how deep his pain ran, knew how much he loved his younger sister, the only family he had left.

'It's only temporary, she'll get better,' she said.

'Maybe,' Early answered, like his mind was on something else.

They had rolled Lisa's chair into the back of the customised van. Music was playing low but no one was listening anyway. In the front seat, Booker looked even blanker than usual. He turned to glance at Lisa, very still, her eyes staring straight ahead through the tinted window.

'I don't like to see her like that,' he said in his deep voice. 'We gotta find who done her like that … then I'm gonna take my time with them.' Booker stopped, shaking his head.

Quite a speech for someone as quiet as him. The big man was more a family member than just a bodyguard. His family and Early's had been close for many years back home. Booker had known Lisa since she was a twelve-year-old kid, when she came to live with their father after her mother died.

'There's the place, Early,' Ice called out.

He parked across the street from the restaurant with the name written in fancy letters on a red, white and green background. The place had been closed earlier on when Ice and Booker had checked it out, but now a black Lincoln was parked in front of the entrance. Early was looking at the front windows silently. Net curtains blocked the view. There was a frame with what looked like a menu list on one side of the door, a poster on the other.

'I check it out?' Booker asked.

Early shook his head. It was best to play it easy, find out more about the place, so

Booker had to be kept on the bench for now. The fact that Lisa had a paper napkin from the restaurant wasn't proof enough, yet something was telling him these were the people behind his sister's shooting. The information Marylee had gotten from Dr Willard seemed to confirm this. It was all starting to make sense.

Ice had people find out more about the people running the place. With Italians, it was better to know exactly what the set-up was, as it was more than likely that the business was mob connected. That wasn't gonna stop Early. This was personal, but he needed to find out the whole story before launching his attack.

'I'll go and check out the set-up...' Marylee offered, waiting for Early's reaction.

'This is a tight play, these guys are probably heavy duty,' Ice remarked. 'If they rough you up, it's on.'

'I'll just play a part, see who's in there, all right?'

The girl was brave, Early knew that, but Ice was right: better play it tight. Yet if someone could get results here it was Marylee.

'What you think, Early?' Ice was waiting for his cousin's decision.

'All right, you're on, miss, but you just go easy, don't push it, OK? Have a look, do it lightly, OK? Don't try and get inside. We pick you up around the corner.'

'Don't worry, I'll be light.' Marylee smiled at Early reassuringly. She made a face at Ice, then quickly undid the scarf covering her hair, then took off her sweatshirt. Now in a Fubu Vest, she scrambled her hair then tied it atop her head with the folded scarf.

'I need to borrow your glasses,' she told Ice.

Her man frowned.

'What you need my glasses for?'

'It's part of my character, OK? Come on, Ice, you'll get them back.'

'I better. Them glasses cost me over two hundred bucks.' Sighing, Ice took off his designer sunglasses and handed them over.

Marylee put them on.

'I'll try and draw them out for you. But how you gonna know if Lisa recognises somebody? She can't talk.'

They all turned to the young woman, still staring vacantly through the van window.

'If she sees the people who hurt her, I'll know,' Early said.

Marylee started to open the sliding door.

'Don't overdo it now, girl. I don't want to have to come out blazing to cover your butt!' Ice called out to her.

One hand on the handle, Marylee turned and grinned at him.

'Be cool, Ice; I'll play it light.'

Then she was out, crossing the avenue against the busy traffic, her slender frame sliding between the passing cars. Early got up and came to stand right by Lisa, passed one arm around her shoulders.

'I don't know if you can hear me, Lizzy ... but you just watch that place now. See if you remember something.'

He couldn't tell whether his sister knew what he was saying, but her eyes seemed glued to the restaurant windows across the road.

Both hands flat against the plate glass, Marylee was peering through, but the net curtains didn't allow much to be seen. Even to her people watching from inside the van, she looked like a different person. Standing back to look up at the colourful sign above, then peering inside again, apparently edgy, Marylee seemed to be talking to herself. Arms flaying up and down, the girl held her head with both hands, then struck a perplexed pose, hands on her hips. The cold wind didn't seem to bother her. She shook her head, spun around on the spot to scan the whole street before coming back to the restaurant.

This time she pressed the doorbell, then again. She did it twice more before a shape appeared on the inside, that of a man in a white shirt and dark apron, big built and bald. Marylee was moving her hands up and down on the sidewalk, saying something, but the man made a gesture that meant 'Go away'. He left. Marylee got back to ringing the bell insistently. The man came back to the door, looking more agitated this time. He must have been swearing, the way he was shaking his finger at the small woman making signs at him from the other side of the door. Eventually he made to open the door, but Marylee didn't move, kept pointing and waving her hands.

By the time he had opened it and got out, she was already ten yards away, still talking to him, looking unsteady on her feet but determined to keep it going.

The man took a few more steps, looking like he was threatening her. Marylee backed away slowly, then turned and move away like she was leaving. None of the passers-by seemed interested in the exchange; worst incidents than this happened every day in New York City, and no one wanted to get too close to problems that didn't concern them. The big man shook his head and got back inside, locking the door behind him.

Inside the van, they were all watching. Lisa showed no reaction to the scene, although her eyes seemed focused on the restaurant. They saw Marylee turn and walk back to the place. A couple of doors away, she stopped at a doughnut stand and searched her jeans pocket for change.

'What she doing?' Booker asked, intrigued.

'Maybe she hungry …' Ice said, but his tone wasn't convincing.

Marylee had bought a bagful of doughnuts and was now ringing the restaurant bell once again. Then the girl calmly took out two doughnuts which she smashed over the parked Lincoln windscreen. Ice, Early and Booker watched in amazement as she went around the car, calmly crushing the fresh jam doughnuts all over it.

'Oh, no!' Ice said, shaking his head in disbelief.

She was on the other side when the man got to the door and lifted the curtain to behold the crazy scene. He looked real mad now, talking and trying to open the door at the same time. Marylee was waiting for him, across the bonnet of the now decorated car, the three doughnuts left in her hands. The door had barely opened before one expertly aimed doughnut flew over and hit the man right in the face.

'Shit!' the usually impassive Booker exclaimed.

Marylee didn't wait for the man to wipe his face and come after her. In rapid fire, she flung the two remaining doughnuts towards him as, now yelling, he came towards her. He moved sideways but not fast enough to avoid one hitting him on the shoulder. He scrambled forward after the girl. The last doughnut was already in the air and hit the glass panel just as another man was coming out. This one was small in stature, wearing a dark suit and with a thin moustache. He looked at the car, incredulous, then at his fat friend trying to follow a slim, dark girl darting through the moving traffic.

Inside the van, Ice was following Marylee's flight towards the corner of the block. He wasn't worried but rather stunned by the inventiveness and courage of his girl. Booker turned from the street drama to looked at Early. He was watching Lisa intensely, watching her breathe hard, her eyes stuck on the little man across the road. Her hands were still flat against the arms of the wheelchair, but he placed one finger on her pulse: it was racing. Early softly brushed his sister's cheek with his fingers, placed his lips against her ear.

'Be cool, Lizzy baby ... I'll take care of that.'

Ice watched the fat man with the apron give up the chase and walk back to the doughnut-covered car. He talked excitedly with the little man in the suit for a few minutes, both making many hand gestures and no doubt voicing heavy invective against the black girl who'd spoiled the vehicle for no reason at all. As soon as they got back inside, Ice started the van and slid into the traffic, taking the right turn at the corner. They found Marylee waiting next to a news-stand, shuffling on the spot to keep warm.

'Girl, you getting more and more crazy!' Ice shook his head as she got inside.

Marylee handed him back the glasses, put on her sweater and fixed her scarf the way it was before.

'When you play a role, you got to get deep into the character,' she commented calmly, and sat next to Early.

'That's what you call playing it lightly...?' He smiled at her.

Marylee shrugged, then asked:

'Anything?'

Early just nodded, his hand still on his sister's arm. 'We'll be back later, for a take-out.'

Why oh why did he marry her? What did he ever find attractive about her? Louis Burrows leaned back in his chair and rubbed the back of his neck. He closed his eyes and tried to unwind. No matter how hard his day, and how much grief he suffered in the crazy job he had, a phone call from his ex-wife Linda was always the worst thing that could happen. It had been a difficult week, and then Linda's late call had made it very much worse. Since their acrimonious divorce, she had been trying to find ways to keep the custody battle going, just to make his life difficult, Burrows felt.

As usual, the call was sweet and sour, Linda resorting to threats and invectives when her attempt at seduction failed.

Burrows stretched and tried to get his mind focused on something more positive. The office was deserted at this late hour. Apart from Maxwell, the black janitor who came every evening, they had all left. Most of Burrows' colleagues would stop at the local cops' watering hole, the Pen, before eventually dragging themselves home to their wives. Run by a retired cop named McShane, the Pen was your typical smoky, macho, after-hours drinking den where policemen from the precinct ended their shift. Most of the guys had a drinking habit, though most would never admit to it. This wasn't California, where even cops were into self-awareness and therapy. This was old, gritty and grey New York, Brooklyn to be precise, a place where cynicism was the norm and drink was the fuel. Drugs habits among cops were by no means uncommon but tended to be wilfully overlooked.

Burrows had lived like that for ten years, drinking first to unwind and forget for a while the street and its woes. Then he found that he didn't really feel like leaving the Pen, knowing full well that Linda would be waiting to complain about some real or imaginary wrong he'd done her.

When their daughter was born, at first

Burrows would come home straight from work. That little wriggling baby had him fascinated, and he'd spend all his time watching her, even when she slept. He really felt that having a child would temper Linda's natural tendency to feel depressed and insecure. And she did seem to change, at least for the first year. But then she got back to her old self, nagging, endlessly complaining and generally trying to drop the weight of the world on her husband's weary shoulders. So Burrows got back into the habit of stopping at the Pen before heading home, staying later and later until eventually it became clear that Linda and he had no other option left but to part.

'How's it going, Max?' Burrows called out to the janitor who was taking time out to have a cup of coffee from the dispenser.

'A'right.' Maxwell nodded, looking up from his newspaper.

Burrows got up and walked to the window. It looked dark and windy out there, cars zooming up and down past the building, a bunch of kids hanging out in front of the deli across the road, posturing and gesturing at passing girls, teenagers on a Friday-night search for fun.

'How's the family?' Burrows asked, coming across to where Maxwell was sipping from a Styrofoam cup.

The man had placed the cup right at the

corner of the paper-filled desk, careful not to disturb anything.

'Not too bad, y'know. Just the usual trouble with my boy.' Maxwell had had trouble with his eldest son since for ever, as far as Burrows could recall. He'd helped him out a couple of times when the boy had started boosting cars and smoking pot, as many neighbourhoods kids do. But now he was into bigger things, burglary and stick-ups, Burrows couldn't help.

'What about your little girl, Max? She doing OK?'

'Well, she ain't little no more. She moved out last month, gone to stay with friends of hers out in Mount Vernon. Left school too! She said she gotta get paid. Ain't looking for no job either, said she's running a business. Don't ask me what kind!'

Maxwell shook his head, took another sip of the hot coffee. Burrows remembered a sweet, ponytailed, dark young girl with dolly's eyes. It must have been a few years back...

'What about your girl? Still in school?' Maxwell asked.

'Yeah, doing all right too.' Burrows nodded, aware that any mention of his daughter was liable to provoke stinging flashes of the mother.

Rhonda Miller's desk, where Maxwell sat, was piled up with files, brown-covered court documents, ID photo folders and all sorts of letters. If it is true that women are generally more tidy than men, Rhonda's desk clearly showed her to be an exception to the rule. That said, it would have been hard to find a New York City cop's desk which wasn't a mess. This was no desk job, after all, and paperwork simply bugged most cops.

In the far corner was a stack of documents no different in any way from the others, but the topmost file caught Burrows' eye. It looked like the one he'd given Rhonda a couple of days before, a yellow file, yellow being the colour code for identification queries. Rhonda had been on her way to the records room when Burrows had asked her to check something out for him. Things had been so busy for both of them that he had not really had time to get back to her, but now the file was sitting there, a brown envelope clipped to it.

Burrows stretched out his hand and picked up the file. He took out the photograph from inside the envelope and frowned. Opening the file, he found the other photo, the one he'd given Rhonda, a black-and-white close-up shot of a battered, bandaged face against a white pillow. Once more, Burrows looked at the other one, a street picture taken with a zoom lens apparently. The young woman in it was leaning against a car, dark glasses covering her eyes, a bandanna tying up her long dark hair. She had on a vest and baggy shorts. Blurred people in the background, all with short sleeves and light clothing, confirmed that the shot must have been taken somewhere warm. It looked like Cali, or Florida maybe.

Burrows left Maxwell to his paper and got back to his desk. At the back of the picture, on a sticker, he read: Lisa 'Jessie' HANLEY – I.R. The two initials, Information Required, indicated that Archives had the person connected to known criminals but didn't possess any details other than a picture and a name. Burrows scratched his left cheek, like he always did when confronted with a problem, and placed the picture against the tall coffee mug on his desk.

At first, he wondered if the two photos were of the same girl. The hospital shot didn't show much of the face; the eyes were closed, the head wrapped and the jaw deformed and wired shut.

Burrows closed his eyes and thought back to the hospital room, to the only time he had actually looked at the wounded girl. He spent a few seconds like that, very still, scanning through his visual memory records until... There it was!

He knew he had clicked on to something that day but he hadn't consciously remembered it. Years of looking at dead bodies, looking for clues and signs, do that to you. It hadn't been obvious that day because of the damage done by the bullet that had shattered the girl's left cheek, but Burrows had recorded the detail. A quick search through his top desk drawer and he retrieved what he was looking for. With the photo flat in front of him, Burrows applied the magnifying glass to the girl's face, focusing on the left side. He had been right: just as in the hospital, the lower left earlobe was missing. It looked like it had been cut off, very neatly. Fortunately, the bandanna was keeping the hair away from the face in the shot, and the wound was visible. So the missing girl who had survived the seven shots was Lisa Hanley ... Burrows nodded and sighed. He was getting somewhere.

Leaning back, he started spinning the name in his mind. Somehow it wasn't unknown to him. Slowly, he went through the few bits of information he had on the young woman. She had been shot and left for dead in a tough Latino area, the fingertips had been burned to prevent identification, she had vanished from the hospital, probably kidnapped... One thing was for sure, Hanley wasn't a Puerto Rican name, so his first assumption about the girl's origin had been wrong. Whoever had dropped her there must have had good reasons to do so.

Burrows remembered Staff Nurse Watts telling him they had found nothing on her and made a mental note to try to get to see her clothing; they might have missed something.

It was getting close to 8 p.m., and his tired mind was longing for closing time, but Detective Louis Burrows was known as an obstinate, almost obsessive cop. Very methodical in his work, he liked to unravel mysteries, tangle with clues, dig up leads when there were none. You have your average cop, using his intelligence and knowledge of the street and the underworld to deal with a case. It's what he does, that's his job. Then you have the hound, the tracker, the detective for whom every unsolved crime is a personal challenge, who goes about finding bits of information as so many clues in a crossword puzzle.

Burrows, though not the only cop with a psychological approach to his work, had this unique perspective on crime in that he liked to become the criminal, to search for the mindset that the perpetrator was in when committing his deed. He liked to tell his colleagues, who marvelled at his ability to solve cases, that he was only a psychoanalyst who had sacrificed a career to make his home town safer.

One touch of his forefinger woke up the computer, brought the screen up. Entering the search programme linked to the police central processor memory bank, Burrows typed the name Hanley and waited. Within fifteen seconds, a list of around sixty Hanleys popped up on the monitor. All Burrows had to do now was proceed by elimination. Some of the names he could discard by memory, but the others required their records to be called up and checked to verify whether they were connected to his search.

The name could be a false lead – it could be a married name. But then she was on file, so there had to be something about her.

Halfway through the list, having reviewed records of all types of criminal activities committed by various Hanleys without finding any obvious relation to the girl in the picture, Burrows decided that his brain needed the sting of a dose of caffeine if it was to keep working properly. He got up and headed for the machine in the corridor. Hot black coffee, the fuel of hard-working cops, the legal drug that helps so many overtaxed police brains ... Burrows burned his tongue with the first sip, and felt all the better for it.

'They should hang 'em!' Maxwell said as he passed by.

'What's up, Max?'

Maxwell looked up from his newspaper, frowning.

'You can't arrest people like that, just shoot them down like dogs.'

Burrows stopped to glance at the paper – a large picture of armed, helmeted policemen looking at five bodies lying on the ground in front of a house. The cover of the Jamaican *Gleaner*. Two of the bodies seemed to be teenagers.

'What's the story?' Burrows asked, too busy to bother reading the article.

'This guy was witness to a murder, so they killed him and all his family. Some vicious beasts, these people!'

Maxwell sounded disgusted. Though he'd left his native Jamaica as a child over forty years before, the janitor read every item of the island's weekly newspaper religiously. He said something else but Burrows wasn't listening to him any more. Something had clicked in his well-trained brain, a connection had just happened, triggered by Maxwell's remark. Jamaica... That was it! That was where he remembered it from!

Burrows dashed back to his desk and started working on his computer feverishly. There were about thirty more Hanleys to go through, but now he knew exactly which one he wanted. He typed: 'Hanley, Dexter', waited for the microprocessor to establish the electronic link to the databank and select the information requested...

Twenty seconds later he was on the

screen. Dexter Wilfred Hanley, aka William Norris, aka Robert Brown, aka Alfonso Johnson, aka Willie Cat, aka Stylee. The photograph showed a well-groomed, smiling, thirty-something dark-skinned man with a perfect set of teeth and fine features. He could easily have been a movie or show business star. However, the thin scar that ran from his left eye to the middle of the cheek would probably have confined him to bad-guy roles in dark thrillers. Burrows knew the story well, having followed it two years previously when the media heavy coverage. But he still printed the file, settled down with his coffee and started to read it over again.

Around the same time, across the river, Tommy was busy gulping the last few forkfuls of a plate of osso bucco in the kitchen of the restaurant. His stomach now full, he wiped his mouth with a napkin then grabbed the wineglass next to him and emptied it. He felt good now. The kitchen was busy at this time. Friday nights were especially good for business. That was when the old friends usually came down to eat and meet at the end of the business week. Saturday was cabaret night, drawing a different, more mixed crowd. But Friday was for the *amici*. On that night, management reserved the right to refuse entry, as they say, which meant that you had to be a little tanned with dark hair to have any chance of getting in. On Fridays, a lot of old-timers frequented the Sciachitana, happy to feel at home there, among friends, free to relax and enjoy authentic cuisine just like it tasted in the old country. Friday was their night.

These days, old man Scaffone hardly ever came down from his suburban retreat, but if he happened to make the trip to old Brooklyn, maybe twice a year, it would be on a Friday. Sal was running the place now and that was all right by everyone. The old guys knew he treated them with the respect due to them, and the newer roosters kept to their side of the room. Though members from different families usually met at the restaurant, there was never any bad feeling shown there. Whatever axes they might have to grind, they left in the cloakroom. The Sciachitana was neutral ground, thanks to the respect unanimously paid to Giuseppe Scaffone.

'Hey, Tommy! Guess who's just arrived.' Paulie walked through from the dining room with his tight little smile.

'I don't know. Who? President Bush?' Tommy answered, straight faced.

'President Bush! Very funny! No, Luigi Tortella!'

Tommy frowned.

'Luigi Tortella? You kidding me? He's doing a twelve in Arizona.'

Paulie shrugged.

'Right. Well, they let him out, he got parole.'

'Parole? How he get parole? They had him down for two counts, I heard!'

'He said he appealed and his lawyer got him out on a procedural point, something like that, I don't know,' Paulie replied, enjoying Tommy's look of disbelief.

'That's what I call a lawyer! Maybe I should meet him, you never know.' Tommy got up, shaking his head. 'Can you believe it? Luigi's out!'

The two men left the kitchen and entered the dining room, where a festive atmosphere already reigned.

Ice waited for the departing vehicle to move out and slipped his van into the empty space. Next to him, Early had his eyes set on the restaurant across the road, watching a bunch of people about to enter the place. Three men in dark suits plus a couple of young women, probably not their wives, the way they acted all high and giggly. The doorman, a mean-looking character, tall and wide, nodded politely as one of the men slipped him a note and opened the door for them.

'I checked around; this is a mob place, no

question,' Ice said, lighting up the half-blunt he'd been holding. 'There's even a private club downstairs. Members only, you know what I mean?'

'Yeah?' Early sounded like he was thinking of something.

'Hmm.' Smoke rose up in the cabin with the sweet odour of the herb and tobacco mix. '–Belongs to Scaffone, head of one of the biggest New York families. The old man's retired now. His nephew runs the place.'

Early nodded, seeming like he wasn't interested, but Ice knew he'd taken in the information. He turned and asked:

'What Lisa doing in a mob place?'

'I don't know. Maybe she felt like eating Italian, a pizza or something...'

Ice regretted saying that as soon as he finished speaking, but Early simply looked at him like he hadn't heard.

Finally, Early shook his head, his face showing deep concentration.

'Lisa's due to come home with the money on Sunday. She ends up in hospital almost dead and the money has disappeared. We find a napkin from a mob place in her car. And she recognised somebody working in there. What d'you think?'

'I think it's clear the hit comes from in there.' Ice motioned towards the brightly lit place on the other side of the road. 'But we need to know if the hit comes from the boss or the soldiers.'

'Why? Dem all the same fuckers. We know they hit Lisa and robbed her, that's all we need to know.'

Ice made a face through the smoke.

'It's not that simple with mob guys. We can't just start an all-out war with them in New York. We want the man behind the hit and the money back, right, Earl?'

'Yeah, that's exactly what we want.' Early's eyes were focused on the restaurant once more. 'And I think we just got someone to help us with that.'

Ice looked across and saw the little guy from earlier on leaving the restaurant. Before he had opened his car door, the blunt was already stubbed out in the ashtray and the van engine was raring to go.

Paulie was late. Sal didn't like people to be late, and Paulie knew that. It was Luigi Tortella's fault in a way; he had bought a round of drinks, then another, and they had all started talking like old friends who haven't seen each other for years do. Paulie had worked with Luigi for a couple of years before the latter got sent to Vegas to work. He liked Luigi, a stand-up guy, a little crazy but a dependable partner. But now Luigi was downing more whiskies down there while he, Paulie, was trying to push his way through the Brooklyn Friday-night traffic to pick up Sal on time.

That weekly run to Queens was something Paulie didn't enjoy at all. He was never comfortable outside his area. Sal was sticking some broad whose old man was doing a ten-year stretch at Rykers. The fact that the guy was one of Sal's soldiers didn't matter to him; the guy was getting his dues and didn't want for anything in the pen. Working out his woman was kind of an extra service Sal was doing for him in a way. Like he'd told Paulie once, if he didn't do it, some other guy would: might as well keep it in the family. Paulie thought it was a funny joke. But there was nothing funny about being late tonight. Sal had a very difficult character at the best of times, and lately, with this DEA business hanging over his head, it was best not to get on his wrong side. Yet he might not be that late, otherwise Sal would already have called him on the mobile. A couple of times he had had to wait over an hour outside the woman's house until Sal had finished bonking her. Paulie relaxed a little. He honked his horn at a slow-driving Buick and overtook it. The woman driver stuck her finger out of the window at him as he passed her. Just another friendly New York night.

A couple of cars behind, Ice was keeping

track of his target without trouble. The van had an eight-cylinder engine that purred like a tiger and leapt like a kangaroo when called upon.

'Looks like he's heading out of town,' Ice remarked.

'And he's in a rush,' Booker said.

He changed the CD in the player and Busta Rhymes's gravelly voice boomed out inside the cabin. Then they watched the Lincoln signal right to catch the exit to Queens.

'We got him now.' Ice smiled.

'Find a quiet spot, we gonna pull him up,' Early instructed him.

They followed the black car for another five minutes until it turned right into a side street that ran alongside the railway line. The traffic there was light, the road bordered by two-storey houses. They were now directly behind the target.

'We gotta do it quickly. He must have noticed us by now,' Ice said.

Early nodded, turned to his soldier at the back.

'Booker, we're taking his car. You jump out and deal with him. Make him sleep, but don't hit him too hard, all right?'

Booker listened to the instructions and simply nodded. He took a pair of surgeon's gloves from his jacket pocket and went to squat by the sliding door, ready to go.

'OK, Ice, do your thing,' Early said.

Swiftly, the van sprang forward and overtook the Lincoln, cutting sharply in front of it. Braking hard, the car bit on the grass verge and stopped. Booker was already out of the van before the driver realised what was happening. All in one, he wrenched open the door and smacked a hard right hand into Paulie's chin just as he was about to say something. Then Booker pushed Paulie's limp body to the other side and took his place behind the wheel. Ice drove off, Booker followed in the Lincoln. The operation hadn't taken more than thirty seconds and there were no witnesses.

'Ice, we need a quiet place to talk with our friend,' Early said.

Ice nodded and picked up his mobile phone.

'I can get you that right in this neighbourhood, not too far from here.' He was already dialling.

'Good,' Early said. 'Let's go there.'

'I'm surprised you guys don't know anything about her. The Bureau's supposed to have the best files on everything and everyone.

Burrows' sarcastic tone wasn't lost on the two agents.

Bronski shrugged. 'We only knew about the two boys. None of the reports ever mentioned Hanley had a daughter.'

'I didn't say she was his daughter,' Burrows pointed out. 'She could be his niece or something.'

Bronski and Carter had responded to Burrows' call immediately. Despite the late hour, both were impeccably dressed. City cops always used to joke that Feds never took off their pants to sleep...

'Jamaicans usually father a lot of kids all over the place,' Carter commented, like he was an authority on the subject.

'You're right: it is the same girl.' Bronski was still checking the two shots.

'So, what does it all mean?' Burrows asked.

Neither of the two FBI agents answered for a while. Down below, a police siren erupted, shrill and aggressive, fading as the vehicle sped away. Then Bronski said:

'A DEA agent disappears at Sal's place and the only potential witness happens to be Dexter Hanley's daughter. The next day, the girl gets shot and left for dead. Two days later, she disappears from the hospital... It's hard not to see a bigger picture.'

'There's definitely a bigger picture here.' Carter nodded knowingly.

'So, what do you think the girl was doing in that place?' Burrows asked, looking at both agents in turn.

'That's precisely what's bugging me,'

Bronski said. 'No way she came in as a customer, not alone anyway. That means she had to be with one of the guys.'

'This is a family place, where those mob guys like to get together and feel at ease. Sometimes they bring their wives. None of them would bring a girl down there, especially a black one,' Burrows pointed out to him.

'He's right,' Carter said. He made a face then added: 'But if she's related to Hanley, anything is possible.'

'Right. She's a long way from Miami and I'm sure she ain't no tourist!'

Burrows rubbed his eye. He should have left the office long ago and gone for a beer, but somehow he felt curious about the girl. He asked:

'What exactly happened with Hanley? It was all over the papers at the time but I always felt they didn't have all the fact...'

Neither of the two agents answered at first, then Bronski shook his head.

'Facts? We had a whole team from the Bureau working on that case for over two years, but even now I'm not sure we got all the facts.'

'Hanley made a deal with you guys, right?'

Carter looked at Bronski, like he needed an OK before talking, then he said:

'That's what we had; a deal. But it didn't work out in the end. Personally, I think

Hanley strung us along from the start.'

'I feel that way too,' Bronski said. 'Old Dexter never had any intention of testifying.'

'But he signed a sworn affidavit against his former partner, didn't he?'

Bronski shook his head.

'Yeah, that's what made us believe he would go all the way. But what we didn't know was that it was a set-up from the start.'

'How's that?'

'Hanley had a sheet as long as a graduation list; extortion, racketeering, drugs, murder, immigration offences ... you name it, over three states – that's what got us on his case. He never got convicted of anything. Witnesses either disappeared or became dumb and blind. But the heat got too much for him in Miami, so Dexter went back to Jamaica. We pushed the case for over a year, and finally we got the Jamaican government to arrest him and issue a deportation order. We went down there and met him, offered him a deal: he gave us evidence against his rivals in Miami and we'd get him on a witness protection programme. His first son had just been murdered by another Jamaican gang in Orlando. We really felt he was out for revenge.'

'What happened?' Burrows asked after several silent seconds.

Bronski seemed to be reliving the story in his head.

'You see,' he resumed eventually, 'Dexter Hanley was one of the most dangerous men I ever came across. And I don't mean crimewise. I mean, you spend an hour with Hanley and he could almost make you believe he'd been the innocent victim of circumstances all along. I've never met someone as intelligently devious as this man. A real actor, old Dexter.'

'So he recanted later on.'

Carter let out a short, bitter laugh.

'Oh no he didn't. But the week after he signed with us, twelve of the top men from the rival gang got murdered, a real St Valentine massacre. Hanley simply got his rivals wiped out in a single night, and all that from the safety of his prison cell in Jamaica. We had nothing but a useless piece of paper with the Bureau's letterhead and Hanley's signature on it. And his lawyer had a copy of it, of course.'

'So he couldn't be touched for the murders but could still claim immunity from prosecution on the basis of his sworn and signed testimony,' Burrows added with a knowing smile.

'Almost. Hanley was still wanted on a gun smuggling charge, big quantities over a three-year period. This wasn't part of the original deal, a little smartass play by the

Miami DA. So we started the deportation procedures all over again. This time we found that the Jamaican government was dragging its feet in cooperating with us. It seemed quite a few people, Jamaican officials, were involved in the operation somewhere along the line, so they didn't want to see Hanley in front of a US federal judge. They were afraid he might let slip a few names, to save himself from a heavy sentence.'

'The guy was no fool,' Carter confirmed, sounding almost respectful. 'I think a lot of people in high places owed him favours and he was calling them in.'

'Eventually, we got the deportation order and set up the operation to transfer Hanley to Miami.'

'His friends let him down,' Burrows remarked.

'Hanley also had enemies in Jamaica, especially on the other side of the political divide. But he didn't give up. Two days before he was due to travel, his lawyer called in and said he wanted to talk. So we met again, and he said he could give us two names, big names from the island, who had financed his smuggling operation. We thought he wanted another immunity deal but that wasn't it. He said he would take his chances in a US court but he wanted two charges of attempted murder relating to his

109

son dropped.'

'The other one?'

'Yeah, he had this nineteen-year-old kid, the surviving one, who had taken over the running of the family business in Miami. At the time he was awaiting trial for the shooting with intent of two undercover DEA agents. We were interested because the two names he gave us were US nationals of Jamaican origin, but the DEA wouldn't play ball. We got the deal cut after some pressure from our director. Hanley signed, the kid walked and we got ready to ship our man to Miami to face a heavy sentence.'

'He knew he was going down?' Burrows asked.

'Oh yeah, he knew he didn't stand a chance of getting off lightly. Hanley was a smart guy, very deep in his own way, very wise,' Bronski confirmed.

'But he didn't get there.'

Bronski sighed, like he personally regretted what had happened.

'No, he didn't... A couple of miles before the convoy got to Kingston airport, the car carrying Hanley blew up, killing him, the Jamaican police driver and the two FBI agents escorting him. I was riding two cars behind, I guess it was my lucky day. We didn't pick up enough from the four bodies to fill one bag.'

Burrows had read the story but it was

different hearing it from an eyewitness.

'Who do you think set it up?'

Bronski sighed, shook his head.

'We didn't find enough evidence to pin it on anyone. In Jamaica, people simply refused to help us with our enquiries. Privately, some of our informants said high-up people had bought a very well-paid contract to prevent Dexter Hanley from making the trip.'

'Makes sense,' Burrows commented.

There was a brief silence in the room. Carter was looking out at the street. On the computer screen, Dexter Hanley was still smiling. Then Bronski said:

'I even heard some people, Jamaicans, say that Hanley set it up himself. His last card, they said.'

'Crazy, ain't it!' Carter commented tersely.

Sal was furious. Tommy knew better than to make any sound when he was like that. He had worked for the man long enough to know that silence was the best policy when his boss was angry. So he just drove the car, looked straight ahead and kept real quiet. Inside, he felt sorry for Paulie, knowing what was likely to happen when Sal finally got hold of him.

'That fucking guy!' Sal cursed for the twentieth time since getting in the car.

When Tommy had received the call in the

restaurant, he had caught an earful of obscenities before he could explain that Paulie had left long ago to pick him up. Sal was in a foul mood then, but sounded even worse by the time Tommy got to Queens.

Paulie was usually dependable, the one vital quality that ensured a long life when you worked for people like Salvatore Scaffone. So what had happened to him tonight, Tommy was curious to know.

It was fair to say that Sal was having a particularly hard time lately. The police raid had upset him, even though he had gotten away with his play rather neatly. But the botched-up hit on the girl was a bad thing, and her escape from the hospital had him feeling there were other people involved, people he didn't know.

The worst had been the visit to his uncle; Sal had felt like the old man knew everything but was toying with him. The fact that he was his sister's son, a direct blood relative, wouldn't weigh much in his favour if old Giuseppe decided Sal had become a liability. And that was making him real edgy right now. He was so upset in fact that tonight's sex session had been a total fiasco. Sal had been sticking the woman every Friday without fail for almost a year, ever since his good friend Silvio had been sent down for a ten-year stretch. He didn't see anything wrong with taking over Silvio's cat;

she wasn't his wife and a girl with big breasts and buttocks like she had wasn't going to be alone for too long. Someone would have to do the job; might as well be Sal. And he'd been doing just that, working out the girl every week, and she loved it.

Except for tonight. Tonight things had not worked out at all. Sal, for the first time in his ladykiller's life, had been unable to 'stand up and be counted', as it were. The truth was he got hard, as usual, when he entered the apartment and cast eyes on his prey, but then it went down. Completely down. He didn't worry about it at first, and the girl soon got working on him and licked him back into shape. But just as he got ready to do his thing, it dropped again. After an hour of the girl trying every stimulating technique she knew, a seriously vexed Sal had to come to terms with the awful truth: he couldn't get it up! So he got upset with the girl, but that didn't help. She being a full-blooded woman, and feeling frustrated herself, more or less told him something to the effect that she could heal the sick but couldn't raise the dead...

That was when Sal started hitting her. And then he hit her again because she cursed him. She got mad and insulted him further, mocking his lack of virility. At which point Sal got all-out mad and gave the girl a serious beating, flinging everything he could get his hands on at her. When it was over, she was badly bruised and bleeding from the mouth and her place looked like it had been ransacked by a bunch of drug-crazed convicts.

Sal was going through a real bad time, and nothing seemed to make him feel any better. But his driver's disappearance had something really weird about it. Once more, he picked up his phone and called Paulie's number.

'OK, buddy, this is how it works: I ask you a question, you give me an answer. If you're a really nice boy, after I find out what I want to know, I might let you off the hook,' Ice explained, then burst out laughing at his own joke.

The fact that Paulie was hanging from a butcher's hook in the ceiling struck him as quite hilarious. Booker didn't even smile. Early just sat on the hood of Paulie's car; he hadn't said a word since they got to the warehouse. The waterfront place belonged to one of Ice's friends who used it to hold reggae and hip-hop dance parties every month.

Paulie, wet from the bucketful of water Booker had flung at him to wake him up, looking thin and vulnerable in his white shorts, still had the spunk to act brave.

'You know who you fuckin' with, you

fuckin' molyan! You better get me down right now!' he spat angrily.

'Hey, you're a tough guy!' Ice said pleasantly. 'I like tough guys.

Booker was standing to the side, his face as blank as a prison wall.

'What's a molyan?' he asked.

'That's what these guinea cocksuckers call black people. It's not very nice.'

Booker simply looked Paulie in the eyes but said nothing.

'It's not very nice, eh... What's your name, buddy?' Ice asked the prisoner.

'Fuck you!' Paulie cursed.

Ice sighed and shook his head.

'It's really difficult to have a conversation with you.'

He walked over to where they had dropped Paulie's clothing and searched his jacket. He found a mobile phone and a wallet, took out the driving licence.

'Paul Gallineri! OK, like I was saying, Paul; since you don't want to talk to me, I'll let my friend ask you the questions. Maybe you and him will get on better.'

Though his feet were on the ground, Paulie's arms were starting to hurt from being stretched upward. Deep inside he was as scared as a rabbit, but he didn't want them to see that. The well-dressed dark man sitting on the car looked young but seemed to be the boss. Paulie knew enough about

115

dangerous men to see that this was one. The big bald guy with the low beard and the dead eyes scared him the most. He looked like he could have effortlessly crushed Paulie's neck with just one of his large hands. It wasn't wise to get this guy angry.

'What the fuck you want with me?' he asked.

'All right, that's better! Now we can have a conversation like intelligent people.' Ice smiled. 'First question: where was you going tonight?'

Paulie looked at the three men in turn before answering.

'I was going to pick up somebody.'

'Who?'

'My boss.'

'All right.' Ice nodded. 'Who's your boss?'

Paulie took a few seconds to think about it. On one hand he knew he should never give up his boss's name, but on the other hand these guys were not cops and he was in a bind. Sal's name would probably let them know they were making a bad mistake.

'I work for Sal Scaffone. You know who I'm talking about?' Paulie let out with some pride.

Pride is very important when you're almost naked facing three guys bigger than yourself.

'Sal Scaffone,' Ice repeated. 'You know him, home?' he asked Booker.

Booker didn't even bother to answer him. Ice glanced towards Early, still sitting quietly on the car.

'OK, Paul. I know about Sal, but I just wanted to make sure we have the right guy. So, what d'you do for Sal?'

Paulie wasn't feeling so good; not only did these guys know who Sal was but they were after him too! They had to be crazy.

'Come on, Paul; what do you do?'

'I'm his driver, OK?'

'You're the driver, right.' Ice sounded satisfied. 'Just the guy we wanted to talk to.'

He let a few seconds pass, just to unsettle Paulie. 'Now, Paul, I'm gonna ask you this 'cause I don't want to make any mistake. You don't do anything else but drive, right? I mean, you're not a bodyguard, an enforcer or a hit-man. You just drive for Sal, am I right?'

'I told you; I'm Sal's driver. That's all I do, I fuckin' drive, all right?'

'Good, Paul, very good. That means you're not the one we're after.'

Another pause, Ice giving the captive time to find hope in his words.

'Just a couple more questions, Paul, all right? About a week ago, one of Sal's people made a hit on a young woman, a black woman. D'you know anything about that?'

If Paulie's balls hadn't already shrunk because of the cold water and the pain of

117

being hooked up like a quarter of beef, they were shrinking now.

'No, I don't know anything about that,' he replied, but too quickly and too weakly. A glance at the bald giant confirmed Paulie's fear: they didn't believe him.

Ice sighed, shook his head.

'Look, Paul, I'll tell you what we know so we don't waste time playing twenty questions here. We know the girl was at Sal's place last week, we know one of you people shot her and left her for dead in east New York the next day, and we know that hitman was at the restaurant this morning. So, you see, we don't really need you that much.'

Ice wasn't smiling any more. He came closer to Paulie, told him very calmly, 'We didn't hurt you so far, Paul, you can see we're not animals. If it was the other way around, if one of us had shot an Italian girl, you guys would have tortured us to death, you know that.'

His eyes locked on Paulie's, Ice said again, 'Just tell us what you know, Paul, and we'll give you a break.'

But Paulie was scared now, scared because he knew this wasn't about business – it was personal, and he didn't believe he was going to get out of it alive.

'I can see you're afraid, Paul, and you don't want to give up your friend. But no one can help you here, and we'll get your friend anyway. Now, one last question: did Sal order the hit?'

Ice waited, noticed that Paulie had started shaking. He turned to Booker.

'I think you better take over, home. Paul ain't talking to me no more.'

Booker moved towards the back of the warehouse, behind the parked van where the little kitchen was, where they prepared food for sale at the dances. He came back with what looked like a long metal stick, the kind they used at cook-outs to turn over the chicken pieces on a grill. But what Booker was holding with a rag to protect his hand was in fact a cattle-branding poker, its W red from having been heated on the gas stove.

'We couldn't find one with NY letters, so we'll just pretend we're from the West Coast,' Ice said, the joke not sounding much like one.

Booker was standing in front of Paulie now, the poker sticking out from his hand. He said 'Shit' as he noticed Paulie was pissing his white shorts, urine dripping on to the concrete warehouse floor.

'It don't have to go down like this, Paul, but you're gonna talk, one way or the other.'

Just then, like the bell rescuing a battered boxer at the end of a round, Paulie's mobile phone rang. Ice frowned, went to pick it up

119

from the pile of clothing where he'd left it. He looked at the calling number, put the phone in front of Paulie's face.

'Whose number's that?' he asked. The phone was still ringing, and Paulie would have given the world just to answer it.

'Sal's, it's Sal's phone,' he mumbled, his eyes glancing at the hot poker and back.

Ice nodded, cut off the call. His mind working fast, he pressed the touch button for calls received and called up the last number.

'What about that one?'

Paulie looked at the screen, visibly shaky.

'The woman's house, it's Sal's woman's number.'

'OK, good.' Ice switched off the mobile and slipped it into his jeans pocket.

'So, question: did Sal gave the order to hit the girl?'

'I ... I don't know.' Paulie's voice was strained, his gaze darting between Ice, Booker and the poker.

'Wrong answer,' Ice said simply.

The poker hit Paulie's skinny ribcage before he even saw Booker's hand move. A high-pitched scream rose in the empty warehouse.

'Was it Sal?' Ice asked again, cool as a prosecuting attorney drilling a nervous defence witness.

Paulie's face was drenched in sweat. A

dark W was etched into his pale skin, seared in the flesh.

'Yeah ... Yeah ... it was Sal,' he sobbed.

'What's the hit-man's name?' Ice asked.

Paulie's eyes were now riveted on the poker in Booker's hand, which began to move just a little...

'Tommy!' Paulie said quickly.

'I'll help you here, Paul, just confirm, OK? Tommy's the big guy who was with you at the restaurant this morning; about fifty, big stomach, not much hair and a moustache, right?'

Something flashed through Paulie's pain-racked brain and he suddenly understood the doughnut-girl incident from earlier.

'Right, it's him,' he said.

Nothing mattered much to him now except to save himself from further damage from the hot poker.

'All right, Paul. You see, we're getting somewhere now. Tell me; why did Sal want the girl killed?'

Paulie was sweating, breathing hard, his eyes wildly switching from the man with the questions to the man with the stick. He said:

'She was working for the police.'

'That's what he said?'

'Yeah, he said she set him up.'

Early had still not moved from his position. He could have been watching a game on TV the way he was quietly listening

121

to the exchange.

'All right, Paul, one last question: you was driving Tommy on the hit, right?'

This time Paulie started breathing really rapidly, giving himself away even before he answered.

'No... No, it wasn't me. Tommy did it on his own. I had nothing to do with it. I swear.'

Ice shook his head.

'You swear? I know you guys are Catholics but we're not, so it don't mean nothing to me.' He turned to Booker. 'Looks like our friend is suffering from amnesia again.'

'No, please! Don't do it!'

Paulie was moving left and right, pulling on his rope, his shoulder muscles now horribly aching. Booker was looking at the poker in his hand.

'It's gone cold,' he said.

'No, man; it's still hot enough.'

'I'm telling you, it's gone cold. I got to warm it up a little,' Booker insisted.

'Come on, it's still all right. Try it.'

'No. No...!' Paulie yelled.

Quickly, Booker touched Paulie's chest with the W. The driver screamed like he was being skinned alive.

'You see,' Ice remarked, pointing to the shape on Paulie's body. 'I told you it was hot enough.'

Booker shrugged and didn't answer.

'OK, Paul, tell me the truth now; you was

with Tommy when he hit the girl, right?'

Paulie looked like he wanted to faint. His mouth was dribbling and his eyes were dancing like crazy.

'OK ... OK... but I was just driving. Please ... You gotta believe me.'

'I believe you, I believe you,' Ice reassured him, then added:

'But I'm not sure my friend here believes you.'

Glancing at Booker's unconvinced frown, Paulie cried out:

'I swear, I drove Tommy but that's all. I'm begging you, don't hurt me again!'

He was crying real tears, the burns in his flesh stinging, his mind maddened by the fear of more pain.

'All right, Paul, stop crying, be a man. You Italians is always going around like you're tough guys and shit but you don't look that hard to me, I gotta tell you. Now, tell me what happened that night. It was at night, right?'

'Yeah, it was at night,' Paulie repeated, ready to confess to anything that might get him a reprieve from the poker.

'Tell me exactly what happened.'

Paulie was in so much pain by now that he didn't care about anyone else but himself. Saving his own life had become his sole concern.

'Come on, don't be afraid. Tell us how it

happened,' Ice encouraged the little man.

'OK ... all right. I drove Tommy to the girl's place.'

'What place?'

'The hotel ... she was staying at this hotel. Sal gave us the address.'

'That was the night after the police raid, right?'

'Right, right; the night after the raid. Sal had someone watching her. So we went down there and when she came out we followed her car.'

'Where was she going?' Ice asked.

'I don't know. She made one stop ... Tommy said she was heading for the airport.'

'Where? Where did she stop?'

'Where? Hmm ... she stopped down by Uttica ... then she came out and drove out again.'

Paulie didn't catch the quick look Ice gave Early.

'OK. Now tell me, Paul; was the girl carrying a bag?'

'A bag? Yeah, she had a travel bag, yeah...'

'Right. Then what happened?'

'Well...' A quick glance at Booker standing by, then Paulie went on:

'So, we followed her then Tommy told me to block her before the Parkway Belt. So I did, and then Tommy got inside her car and I followed him.'

'And then?'

'Then he drove to this dump place in east New York and left the girl there.'

Ice nodded, paused while Paulie looked left and right, searching for mercy.

'When did Tommy shoot the girl, Paul?'

Paulie's breathing got faster.

'I ... I didn't see him...' He began.

The glance from Ice to Booker was all it took to motivate him.

'OK... OK... He had this gun with a silencer. He ... I think he shot her when he got inside her car.'

'You think?'

'He shot her once ... then he drove her car.'

'Did he shoot her in the head?'

'What?' Paulie asked, bewildered. 'Yeah, he shot her in the head.'

'So, when did he shoot her again?' Ice asked, pressing on. 'Like I said; we stopped by that dump place and Tommy took her out of the car.'

'So you didn't see what happened.'

'No, I didn't see anything.' Paulie sounded relieved to be able to say so.

'And then?'

'Then Tommy came back and we drove off.'

'But you left the girl's car there?'

'Yeah, we left it...' Paulie confirmed. 'Tommy said he had cleaned everything ... he said the police would think it was a story between Puerto Ricans.'

'Yeah. Tommy's a real pro, eh?'

Paulie didn't answer that. Ice came a little closer to him and asked quietly:

'What happened to the bag, Paul?'

'The bag?'

'Yeah... You said the girl was carrying a bag. What happened to it?'

'The bag...' Paulie swallowed and sniffed. 'Tommy took it. He said we shouldn't leave no evidence ... so nobody would know who the girl was.'

'So he took the bag home with him, right?' Ice asked.

'I ... I think so. He dropped me off and went home.'

'OK, Paul; that's all we wanted to know. Now we know you didn't shoot the girl.'

Paulie looked at Ice, then at Booker.

'So ... what happens now?' he asked Ice anxiously.

'Now? Well, I told you if you helped us, we'd give you a break, right?'

'Right... Right.'

Hope was still alive in Paulie's puffed-up eyes.

'We know what we wanted to know.' Ice motioned to Booker. 'Get him off the hook, home.'

Booker put down the poker and yanked the rope up, effortlessly lifting Paulie's body free from the big metal hook. Paulie dropped to his knees like a wet bag.

Early hadn't said a word since they'd got there, but Paulie could feel he was the real boss. So he tried calling on him.

'Look, mister, I drive, that's what I do. I follow orders, that's all. Please, you got to understand.'

'It's OK, Paul; we understand. Don't we, home?' Ice said reassuringly.

Booker didn't even answer. He had just picked up the subtle silent order from Early. This completely escaped Paulie, now begging for his life.

'But he...' Ice told Paulie. 'He won't understand.'

Still on his knees, Paulie looked at Ice, then at Early.

'You see, Paul,' Ice explained, 'that girl Tommy shot is his sister.'

Paulie barely had enough time for the information to reach his brain. He didn't feel Booker's wrestler-size arm fold around his frail neck until it was too late. His cervical vertebrae snapped under the pressure three seconds later. Booker released him and he sank to the concrete floor of the warehouse, dead in his soiled white shorts.

Ice shrugged. 'I said we'd give him a break. I didn't say what kind.'

Booker looked at him blankly.

'Let's clean up and move out,' Early ordered calmly.

Saturday

Springtime was close at hand, no doubt about it. The cold wind that had blown over New York during all of March had subsided, replaced almost overnight by a cool, mellow breeze heralding the change of season. Marylee tasted the soup in the tall plastic cup, satisfied herself that it wasn't too hot. Carefully, she inserted the straw between Lisa's lips.

'Come on, miss, drink this and tell me if I can still cook.' She smiled.

She could feel the pull on the straw as the warm liquid rose up it, passed into Lisa's throat. The previous day, Dr Willard was brought in and checked the wounded girl, deciding that she was well enough to take off the neck brace. Although Lisa still seemed unable to move, Dr Willard had tested her reflexes and was surprised to notice a faint reaction in her right leg. It wasn't anything major, not a real movement, but he said it was a good sign, that there was hope she would recover at least some of her functions. He explained that after a major shock the nervous system sometimes goes to sleep. It might be what had happened with Lisa. He said they would need to get her checked by a specialist to be sure. Marylee told him they would, but later. Early wanted him to come over every two days, alone. Marylee told Dr Willard they only trusted him, so he would have to take care of things for now.

'Take your time now.' Marylee drew out the straw to let Lisa rest. 'Fish tea's good for you. It'll give you back strength. The doctor said you're doing fine. Pretty soon you gonna start to feel sensations in your arms and legs, you'll see. Now, have some more of the soup, slowly now, there you go.'

In truth, Marylee had no idea whether Lisa would fully recover, but even before Dr Willard had said she'd shown some reflexes she had always believed she would. She simply had faith in the power of prayer, and just the fact that Lisa had survived was a sure sign that God wanted her to pull through. It was the way she saw it.

'Right, you've had enough, I can see that. Soon you'll be eating like before. I'm gonna do you some real nice meals, so you can get strong again. You will walk, I know you will, so don't worry about anything. Look how nice it is today! You see them birds on the fence down there? Springtime's coming up, you feel it?'

Although she couldn't be sure Lisa heard what she said, Marylee never tired of talking to her. Dr Willard had tested Lisa's hearing and, although she had not responded positively, he said it was possible she might hear some sounds. In any case, Marylee was convinced she could at least read her lips, so she kept talking and making gestures, while Lisa kept fixing her with that deep stare of hers. It was precisely that spark, that flicker of intelligence, which Marylee was certain she could discern in Lisa's steady gaze, which kept her talking to her silent friend.

The two young women had gotten to know each other well in the two years Lisa had been doing the New York run for Early. She'd come up once a month, spend a few days with Ice and Marylee, then fly back down south with the 'collection'. Marylee had instinctively taken to the tall, slim brown girl with the deep, dark eyes. Lisa seemed quiet, shy even, when you didn't know her, but Marylee soon found out that the girl had the same fearless disposition as her older brother. Like Early, she wasn't very talkative, yet she would always make her mind known when she needed to. But Lisa was cool to hang out with. Marylee, herself an exile from California, had found in Lisa someone with the same easygoing ways as her.

'Lisa, I'm praying for you every day, asking God to give you his blessing, to bring you back like before. I know you're praying too in your heart. You're gonna be all right, girl, I know that.'

Marylee had Lisa's still hands in hers, her eyes on Lisa's eyes. She raised her right hand and slowly, carefully ran her fingertips over Lisa's face, lightly over her wounds.

'Don't worry about a thing, Lisa, you're still very pretty. All the hurt will go away, God will take your pain away.'

A rapper of some fame in her young LA days, Marylee had recognised in Lisa a potential singer of quality, and encouraged the younger girl to put her talent to use. Eventually, earlier in the year, Ice had got Lisa to record a couple of tracks and had been working on them.

She began to sing softly, an old classic love song she recalled her friend singing in the studio to warm up her voice one evening. Marylee could feel the intensity of Lisa's gaze, her features frozen as always yet somehow brighter, as it bathed in the love words of the song. She stopped, smiled at her friend.

'I wish you could sing it for me. You got a better voice than mine.'

She touched her lips with two fingers.

'You'll sing again soon, you'll see.'

The atmosphere in the office was dark. It was barely ten in the morning, but the place was filled with clouds of cigarette smoke mixed with wafts of expensive aftershave. Of the four men seated around the room, none had spoken a word since they had arrived and none was willing to make a sound unless expressly required to do so by the boss. Given the foul mood the boss was in, it would only take the slightest noise to provoke his wrath, and no one wanted to become the target. Behind the desk, a half-finished cigarette in hand and half a dozen stubs in the ashtray, sat Sal, his face a mask of contained fury.

Having spent the first two hours of the morning with FBI agents, for the second morning in a row, Sal was mad. His knitted brow and the twitch in his left cheek made it plain that he was a man with serious worries on his mind. Though his gaze was lost somewhere on the back wall, the men were keeping very still, knowing that Sal usually let fly at anyone when he was in a bad mood. Today was no mood problem, though, today was about a major situation. Things were going seriously wrong for Sal.

The recent string of bad news had culminated this morning in a nightmare: Paulie found dead in his car in Queens with a headless chicken in his lap. That was a vision Sal could have done without, but those FBI cops had found nothing better to do than to drag him out of bed and bring him to the gruesome scene. They seemed to enjoy it all, those bastards. Of course, Sal had told them he didn't know who could have done that. But now, chain-smoking and turning things over and over in his mind, he was coming to the only possible conclusion: his enemies in Queens were taking advantage of his current problems to hit him.

And what was making it worse, he had unwittingly provided them with a reason by beating that girl the previous night. Sal was sure it was all connected. That whore must have run to Luigi's cousin, Fat Massimo Del' Ante, to complain of the beating from Sal. And Massimo, that fat pig, must have thanked God for the opportunity to hit at Sal. He had been waiting for years to make his move, feeling that old man Giuseppe had lost his grip on things and eager to pounce on his territory. Him and Sal had never liked each other, so the fact that Sal was sticking Luigi's girlfriend was a good enough excuse to act. Of course, he suspected, Sal knew that, but he couldn't have moved unless that bitch went crying to him!

'That fat cocksucker!' Sal swore to himself.

The men waited still, knowing their boss was mulling things over before deciding on his next move. Besides Tommy, looking gloomy in the far corner near the window, Joe Capri, Matty Gianco and Angelo Tucci were sitting there. Joe was an oldtimer, just like Tommy, except that he was originally from Chicago. He had come to work for Sal a couple of years earlier after his boss and brother-in-law, Sam the Shark Bossanza, had died of a heart attack while serving time in a minimum-security establishment for a minor conviction. Joe had never believed in the medical report on Sam's death, and his dislike of the new capo had made it urgent for him to leave town. Dark-complexioned and sullen-looking, Joe was built like an NFL quarterback but had the strength of a linebacker. Fast and efficient, he was loyal to Sal for having rescued him, and did whatever his new boss told him to without hesitation. A reliable friend he was.

Angelo Tucci, barely thirty years of age and looking like a college boy, was a distant relative of Sal's he had been asked to find work for by the old man. Brash and talkative, Angelo was your average Italian boy; cocky, quick tempered and with more balls than brains. He had yet to make his bones. Sal had no special love for him, but, family ties being what they are, he had to take care of the kid.

Then there was Matty, counsellor and tutor to Sal, ex-consigliere to Giuseppe Scaffone, whose experience went back to the bad old days of the family feuds. Still in his fifties, lean and impeccably dressed in his usual white shirt and cardigan, Matty didn't smile very often but was known as a man of heart, open to arrangements yet knowing how to show himself merciless when he had to. Although Sal was the decision-maker, he knew that going against Matty's advice was never wise.

'Tommy, you got back the car?' Sal asked, crushing a cigarette end in the ashtray.

'The police said they got to dust it for prints, Sal. We'll get it back this afternoon.'

'When you do, sell it, burn it, I don't care; I don't want to see it again. Get me another car, today.'

'OK, Sal.'

'Joe, you send some guys to check out Fat Massimo's place in Queens. I want to know when he eats, when he sleeps and when he goes whoring and where. You get me a full report on that pig. He wants war, he's gonna get it.'

Matty spoke for the first time since entering the office.

'You need to think things over, Sal; take your time before you make a move.'

Sal's face was a mask of restrained fury.

'Matty, I thought about it, OK. I've been thinking about it so much I got a fucking headache. If you'd seen Paulie sitting there dead with a fucking headless chicken you've had a headache too!'

'Are you sure it's Massimo who did it? We've had no trouble with him for a long time,' Matty pointed out calmly.

'That's because he was waiting for the right time to hit me! I'm telling you he's the one. That girl problem gave him the excuse he needed.'

Matty made a face like he was far from convinced.

'It's not wise to mix in other people's women...' he said, knowing Sal understood he had been wrong in the first place. '...but I don't think Massimo is crazy enough to start a war over that.'

Sal exhaled, frustrated.

'Look, Matty, I have no problem with anybody else. That fat boy has been looking at my territory for a long time. He knows the cops have been after me lately so he thinks I'm weak and it's the right time to make his move. That's what it is.'

He lit another cigarette, grunted.

'But he just made a fucking mistake. I'm gonna wipe out that sonofabitch!'

Tommy shifted in his chair.

'Poor Paulie, he wasn't even packing a gun! These guys are fucking cowards,' he muttered.

Him and Paulie went way back, so the death of his friend had hit him especially hard.

'Why don't you call Massimo, Sal; just to make sure...' Matty suggested in his quiet voice.

'Call him? Call him? Are you kidding me?' Sal fumed. 'Why don't I invite him for dinner?'

He shook his head, sat up in his chair, just about restraining himself, because he was addressing Matty Gianco and he had to stay polite.

'Do me a favour, Matty, just help me wipe out this cocksucker. I know where the hit comes from and I'm gonna defend what's mine. Just don't tell me to talk to him.'

Matty took out a pack of cigarettes, an obscure brand made from dark, odorous tobacco that only he enjoyed, and lit one. After blowing out some smoke, he remarked:

'Maybe you're right, Sal, maybe it's Massimo but nobody's gonna gain from an all-out war. Times have changed.'

'Sure, times have changed, but Paulie's dead, and if I just let it go, tomorrow they'll hit another one of us. I didn't start this war, Matty, you know that.'

Grey clouds were wafting around Matty's greyish head.

'I know, Sal, but the old man wouldn't handle the problem like that. Maybe you need to wait a couple of days, talk to some people.'

One thing Sal never liked was to hear about what old Giuseppe would have done, how he would have handled things. He was the boss now, and to be told that in front of his men wasn't good for his image. He squinted but held back somewhat.

'Matty, I have a lot of respect for you, you know that. And I have respect for the old man. But this is my problem, I have to deal with it, no one else.' Sal paused, made a hand gesture and asked: 'Why d'you want me to talk to people? And who am I gonna talk to? You know the other families only want something like that to happen, so they'll just wait and see who wins then move in on the loser. Right?'

'Right, so why not try and solve the problem peacefully? Talking to his enemies doesn't make a man weak.'

Though he understood and knew it made sense, Sal still wanted his own way. Maybe because he knew he had caused the first offence by going out to plough another man's furrow.

'OK, Matty, we'll talk, but only after I've evened the score with Fat Massimo. He's got to feel hurt, like I feel, then he'll understand he made a big mistake. I want him to cry a little. After that he'll be nice to me, you'll see.'

Matty, the old-time consigliere, he who had lived through real family wars, drew on his smoke.

'*Va bene, Sal, tu sai il capo*,' he said.

The way Matty said that, and the expres-

138

sion that came with the words, should have made Sal think about it. But he was too hot, too hurt in his pride to be level headed this morning. He turned to his men.

'Right. Joe, you and Tommy take a trip to Queens. I want information on Massimo's operations, I want details on his security, find out his weak points. Be careful; he must be on his guard, so just watch out. You go, spy on him and come back and report to me.'

'OK, Sal.' Joe nodded obediently.

'And take Angelo with you.'

Joe got up. Tommy threw Angelo an ambiguous look, as if he wasn't pleased to have him along but couldn't say so to Sal, not this morning.

'And, kid...' Sal called out to his relative. 'You keep your eyes open and your mouth shut, OK?'

'OK, Sal.' Angelo nodded, feeling like he was being elevated to an important position in the family, at last.

The two old hands and the apprentice left the room. Matty seemed absorbed in his cigarette.

'And Tommy!' Sal shouted as the door closed. 'Get me a car on your way out!'

Marylee stopped at the kitchen door and watched in amazement the way Booker was going through his meal. Early had eaten little and quickly, Ice was finishing his last piece of corn, but the big man was still in full swing. In a blue Lakers vest that exposed huge shoulders and biceps like those of a WWF wrestler, Booker had his eyes set on a plate piled up with a couple of pieces of chicken, greens, fries, corn and beans. He munched slowly, almost methodically, not looking around or taking part in the conversation. Food was a serious thing to Booker. When it came to eating, he had no friends. Though he ate a lot compared to the average man, he had his set amount and wouldn't go over it, no matter what. At around 280 pounds, Booker carried very little fat; his body was lean despite the size, muscles only.

His attitude to food stemmed from the rough poorhouse childhood he had endured, roaming the streets of Kingston, hunting for his daily meal wherever it could be found. An orphan at birth, Booker had never known the comfort and security of a family home, never experienced the loving feeling of a mother's arms, aside from the dedicated care of the ladies at the orphanage in his first few years of life. He had survived, though, a scavenger among scavengers in the hot jungle of low-life Kingston. Until his path crossed Dexter Hanley's.

'I'm glad you like my cooking, Booker.' Marylee smiled.

The man took a few seconds off to look up, nodded without a smile.

'Yeah,' he managed between two powerful munches.

'He likes it. You're a wicked cook, miss. Ice lucky,' Early said.

'Well, he doesn't realise it,' Marylee responded with a raise of the eyebrows to her husband, before slipping back inside the kitchen.

'Don't say that, baby, you know I'm mad on you!' Ice called out to her. 'You want a beer, Early?'

'All right.'

Ice went to the fridge and retrieved two beers, plus a maxisize bottle of Jamaican ginger beer Marylee had bought especially for Booker. The man didn't touch alcohol or tobacco.

'Let's go chill in the garden.'

Early and Ice walked through the living room, dropped into two of the wooden reclining chairs lined up on the tiled garden patio. A cool afternoon sun bathed the garden, lighting up the water drops in the fountain.

'You want to taste some chronic?'

Ice had taken out his herb bag and was showing Early some fat light green buds.

'Your sense done?'

'You Yard boys don't like nothing else!' Ice laughed. 'I can get you some later, but try

141

this, man; it's nice and fresh.'

Early picked up two buds and proceeded to roll them in his palm. One sheet of Rizla and the spliff was soon rolled up. Ice preferred the blunt style, chronic wrapped in tobacco leaf.

'Baby!' he called out after the first long pull. 'Play the cassette in the machine, turn it over.'

Shortly after, a crisp drum roll broke through the small Tannoys fixed to the wall above the patio entrance. The rhythm hit them, tight and dry, piano flavoured.

'Check this out; this kid is only sixteen. He voiced the tune last weekend. He's gonna blow up.'

Early listened, impressed by the vocal quality of the young singer. He knew Ice was all music from an early age. He'd spend nights recording and mixing music and had built a reputation as one of the top producers in town. Being Brooklyn born, he was heavily into hip-hop but his origins kept calling him back to reggae music, and he worked with artists from both worlds. The track sounded real promising to Early.

'It's just a rough mix. Wait till I get some polishing on it!'

Ice went on to explain how he had noticed the youngster hustling crack in a backstreet near his studio. One night he had found the youngster bleeding from the head, not seriously hurt but smarting from being robbed at gunpoint by other, bigger hustlers. When Ice had got him inside and patched up, the youngster said he had written lyrics but never done anything with them. At the end of the night, Ice had three songs voiced, thanking God for having sent a new artist his way.

'That's the new kid you recorded?' Marylee asked, joining them outside.

'Yeah. He's bad, right?'

'With a voice like that, he'll go far ... if he don't get wrecked on rock.'

Ice looked at his woman through the smoke around his head.

'Yeah.'

'Booker finished eating?' Early asked her.

'Yeah, he's watching the game on TV.'

When resting, Booker could stay in front of the screen for days on end, it seemed, simply flicking from programme to programme and from channel to channel, until sleep eventually took him over.

'What's up; gimme me some of the chronic, baby,' Marylee asked her husband.

'You know we talked about that before...' Ice replied smoothly.

'Come on, I can take a little draw now and then. I'll be cool.'

'You'll be cool, all right, but it's not about you.' Marylee smiled, shook her head, looked at Early.

'Early, would you tell your cousin here that herb is OK for babies, please?'

'Babies?' Early raised his eyebrows.

'Oh, he didn't even tell you?'

'With all this happening, we didn't get time to talk. I was gonna tell you, man...' Ice explained.

'This man is gonna be a daddy.'

'For real?' Early smiled, maybe for the first time since he'd arrived in town.

'For real.'

'That's cool. But it don't even show!' Early glanced at Marylee's waist.

'Oh, I'm only about three months gone. I'll soon get big, you'll see.'

'That's good news. I'm happy for you. Hey, Ice, you better get serious now.'

'That's exactly what I've been telling him!'

'I am serious, that's why I want her to ease up on the herb,' Ice pointed out.

Early took a deep draw, looked at the spliff, nodding.

'Not bad, your stuff. You know, herb don't hurt babies, she just have to take it easy with it.'

'You see!' Marylee made a face at her husband and father of her child. 'Anyway, you know me, Early; I only take a couple of draws a day, nothing more.'

'You be all right, miss. My mother used to take a draw now and then when she was pregnant, she told me. Just make sure you eat good and rest yourself, your baby be all right.'

Ice sniggered.

'You try to tell this woman to rest. You see the kind of play she gets into, like yesterday at the restaurant?'

'A baby needs action to get strong, that's what my mother told me,' Marylee stated.

'She was as crazy as you are when she was pregnant with you; that's why you're like that too!' Ice said, shaking his head.

'I'll tell her you said that.'

'You can tell her, she knows it's true.'

Early was used to these two mock-fighting all the time. They loved each other but kept teasing one another, and that was the way they liked it.

'Lisa still sleeping?' he asked.

'Yeah, she's all right. That ride in the park did her good.'

'She eat something?'

'Yeah, I made her some oxtail soup,' Marylee explained. 'Soon her wounds gonna heal, she'll be able to eat solid food. She needs lots of rest also.' She paused, knowing Early felt bad about his sister. 'She's gonna recover, don't worry.'

Early didn't answer right away, just stared at the garden wall for a while, then he said:

'I did promise my father I'd take care of Lisa.'

Ice looked at Marylee. He knew Early

blamed himself for what had happened to his sister.

'It's not your fault, Early. She did the run for over a year without problems. Something happened here that's nothing to do with it, and we gonna find out exactly what.'

Early nodded slowly, told him, 'You know, when Wally died, it's only Lisa helped me to overcome it. Then my father died too, and she was stronger than me, she stopped me from going all the way crazy. She was there for me all the time.'

Ice didn't want to let Early dwell on that, knowing two years hadn't been a long enough time for his cousin to really get over both tragedies. He had flown to Miami right away when Early called him to tell him of Wally's death. Still in hospital recovering from two bullet wounds, Early explained to him how his older brother had saved his life by throwing himself over him, covering him with his body when their car was ambushed and raked with automatic fire in Orlando. Wally was hit fourteen times and died on the spot. Early was covered in his brother's blood when they pulled him out. Six months later their father was dead too.

'She's strong, she'll make it ... else she wouldn't have survived,' Marylee said confidently.

Early took a sip from his beer, looked at his cousin's wife.

'I don't know if it's right to say that, miss ... but if she's gonna stay like that, maybe it would have been better she didn't make it.'

Early's words hung in the cool afternoon air for a few minutes, until Marylee spoke:

'I don't know, Early... She's alive and she's fighting. With love from us and prayers, she'll get better.'

'Yeah, man; she's strong; she's a Hanley,' Ice said firmly.

Early inhaled deeply, like drawing courage from the breeze.

'I really hope to God she gets back her legs, because I don't know if she could stand it to live in a chair all her life. I don't want her to give up.'

'She's not gonna give up, she'll fight to the end, you know how she is,' Marylee said.

'Yeah, she'll fight ... as long as there's hope left. But if she finds out she'll never walk again, I'm not sure what she'll do. I don't want that to happen, you understand what I'm talking about...'

Early stretched out his hand and picked up the lighter from Ice's chair arm. He lit up his draw and blew out strongly, as if the thick white smoke could dismiss the negative vibration from his words.

'I'll go and change the cassette.' Marylee left the two men.

It was a promotion, Angelo could feel it.

Though he was sorry for Paulie, the driver's death was offering him an opportunity to get on the team, something he had been hoping and praying for. After spending almost a year running errands for Sal, tagging along with the old hands and generally doing nothing but lowly and insignificant jobs, Angelo was getting his due, at last. It was all well and good to be the boss's cousin, but what he wanted was to be given the chance to prove himself. Sal kept telling him to wait, that he was too green to handle responsibilities, that his time would come. Watch and listen, he'd tell him all the time. But Angelo was getting fed up with that, watching and listening to big men bragging about their deeds. He knew he could hold his own with any of them, he was sure of it, if only he was given the opportunity to prove it. And now there he was, driving a Candy, heading for action, real action. Under his self-assured and cool exterior, Angelo was as excited as a rookie being called off the bench for the first time. Next to him, Tommy smirked.

'Can you believe that broad? Calling Sal to come to her place, like nothing happened!'

From the back seat, Joe Capri cleared his throat.

'I don't get it,' he said

'You don't get it? That's Massimo's hand

behind her. He must think Sal's fucking stupid.'

'But why would he do that? If he killed Paulie, he knows Sal got his message. Why try something stupid like that?'

Joe had a gruff voice like a bear with a sore throat. He sounded puzzled.

'Why? 'Cause he's dumb, that's why!'

'He's got to be dumb to think Sal's gonna fall for a trick like that,' Angelo said, trying to get in.

'Kid, just drive the fucking car, all right?' Tommy told him firmly, then went on: 'Hey, Joe, you know what my old man used to say?'

'No, what did your old man used to say?'

'He used to say that when a man's time has come, he makes a mistake he would never make usually. But he slips, only that one time, because that's the way it's got to go.'

Joe didn't offer any comments on the wise sayings of Tommy's father.

'That's why Massimo's slipping; 'cause his time has come,' Tommy added.

'I still think we should have brought more men.'

'More men? What for?'

'Massimo can't be that easy to get at.'

Tommy turned to look at the ex-Chicago hit-man.

'Joe, you're not listening to what I'm

telling you. We're not going to a shoot-out, we're going on a hit. Massimo isn't expecting us. He sent his best guys to the girl's house, 'cause he thinks we're going to show up there with Sal. He'll be waiting at his bar for the call, that's how he works.'

'So we're just gonna walk in and blast him? It can't be that easy,' Joe said, doubtful.

'It is that easy. Listen to me; I know his place, I've been there a few times some years ago, when old man Giuseppe used to visit Massimo's father. I was taking care of security arrangements. I was just a kid back then, about the same age as Angelo here.'

'Right. That's what I tell Sal all the time; I'm old enough for big things now,' Angelo butted in.

'OK, kid; but for now, just drive and shut up,' Tommy said kindly.

'So you know the place,' Joe agreed. 'But Massimo knows you too, and he's not gonna believe you come over from Brooklyn just to have a drink in his place!'

'Right, but I'm not the one he's gonna see walk in; you are.'

'Me?'

'Yeah. He doesn't know you. You're not from New York, and Massimo doesn't know anyone in Chicago.'

Joe reflected on this for a while, then said:

'But he won't be alone in there.'

'He's gonna have a couple of guys, maybe only one, watching him while he's playing cards. He always plays cards with his friends on Saturday evenings from six o'clock... There's a back door to the bar through a little alley. I'll walk in on them and take care of his boys while you blast him. It's an easy move, don't worry.'

'I always worry before a job, that's why I don't make mistakes,' Joe stated flatly.

'Yeah, well, just let me worry about this one. You just walk in with a big smile, drop him and walk out.'

Tommy sounded totally confident. Joe asked, looking more confused:

'With a big smile? Why d'you want me to smile?'

Sighing like he was trying to get through to a difficult child, Tommy said:

''Cause he's gonna think you're some old friend of his. That'll throw him off for a few seconds. Get it?'

Joe didn't answer, bit his lip like he was thinking it over.

'Very smart, Tommy,' Angelo commented appreciatively.

'Yeah. Just watch your speed, OK? We don't want to get pulled over,' Tommy told him.

As the Caddy slowed down to observe the speed limit, the dark customised van that had been trailing it eased up to let another car overtake. Ice didn't know that Angelo was too excited and inexperienced to check for a tail, like any good mob driver always does. Beside him, Early was watching the road from behind his shades. Used as he was to the wide palm-lined avenues and broadly built, colourful buildings of his native Miami, New York always seemed cramped and overbuilt to him. Even with the orange sun setting over it he didn't see what people could find attractive about the town.

'I wonder who they're going to visit in Queens,' Ice remarked, as if talking to himself.

Chance had it that, as they reached Sal's restaurant to look for Tommy, their target was leaving with two other men. So they decided they might as well follow the hit-man to wherever he was heading and play it as it went. The mission was to kidnap Tommy and interrogate him. To Early, the hit-man was already dead anyway, but he had to retrieve his money from him first. The fact that there were two other guys with him was more like a bonus. They might come in handy when it came to extracting information.

'Queens seems a good place to die,' Early said flatly.

'Yeah ... I like that,' Ice told his cousin.

'You know, it sounds like a good lyric.'

Right away he started improvising on the beat playing in the background:

'Come to Queens, it's a good place to die... Lots of friends to wish you bye-bye... Whether you a big man, or just a little guy... Queens is where your family will come to cry.'

Ice stopped and turned to Early.

'What you think?'

'I think you better stick to producing ... or you'll end up broke.'

'Maybe you're right. I got a good ear for music but my voice ain't all that,' Ice said.

The street hadn't changed much in twenty years. Apart from a fresh coat of paint and a new polished hardwood front door, the bar looked the same as it did when Tommy used to come over with his boss. Back in those days, the place was the focal point for all Italians living in the area, somewhere to enjoy a cup of dark strong coffee or a glass of fruity-tasting wine from the old country. Massimo's father had opened the place soon after emigrating to America and operated it himself for over thirty-five years. Even after he had become the capo of all the borough of Queens, he'd still be serving his friends from behind the bar. They had parked a little way away, across the street.

'OK; give me a couple minutes to go

around the back, then you go in. I'll cover you while you hit Massimo,' Tommy told Joe. 'Kid, when Joe tells you, you do a U-turn and park right in front of the door, OK?'

'OK, Tommy.' Angelo nodded, trying not to look too excited.

'No wild driving, OK; just turn it around and park, leave the engine running. You got that?'

'Yeah, yeah.'

'Joe's going in, then we both coming out by the front door. We're using silencers, so there won't be no noise.'

'Maybe I should have a piece too, just in case you need help...' Angelo said, looking at both men in turn.

Tommy smiled and shook his head, motioned to Joe.

'You believe that kid?... Just keep calm, kid, I got it all worked out.'

Tommy checked out both sides of the street again, scanned the front of the pleasant-looking café with tall potted plants either side of the door. The place didn't seem protected; no one outside and the two cars parked in front were empty. Keeping his hands low, he pulled out his gun from his coat and checked it. Satisfied, he replaced it.

'OK, Joe, you wait two minutes until I get in through the back, then you come in, all right?'

'All right, two minutes then I go in.' Joe nodded.

'Right. Let's do it.'

Tommy opened the door and left the car. Mingling with the early Saturday evening crowd, he crossed over and walked down the avenue, turned into the little alley lined with metal rubbish bins and empty crates. At the far end, he found the same old rickety wooden gate that led to the back yard, where beer casks used to be delivered and stored. First checking he wasn't watched, Tommy walked on, heading for the back door.

He got there and froze: a locked iron-bar gate blocked the entrance. Tommy's brain took in the obstacle that ruined his perfect plan and switched off for a few seconds. The door behind the gate was half open, and beyond the small kitchen area he could make out the barman behind the counter, thin and tall with a bald pate, talking with a younger man, suited and wearing shades. Beyond the bar, to the right, several men were seated, throwing cards on a table. Massimo's bulk and head of curly grey hair were visible. Tommy didn't know the two older guys playing but the third one he recalled very well; Leonardo Loria, ex-first gun to Massimo's father and Tommy's old nemesis. Leonardo was smiling and throwing down a good card. Tommy couldn't see the front door from where he was, unless he pushed his hand through the gate and swung it back farther, but if it squeaked it might draw attention to him.

He heard a noise and knew someone had walked in from outside. His heart sank as he saw Joe walk towards the card players. Instinctively, Tommy drew out his gun. From his position, he could try taking out the man with the shades, Massimo's bodyguard apparently. The others wouldn't be carrying. But it wouldn't be a sure shot. His heart in a vice grip, Tommy watched Joe walk past the bar; the guard threw him a side glance and kept talking to the bartender. Tommy frowned. Joe walked on towards the table, and Tommy realised what was wrong: Joe's hands were not in his pockets but just hanging alongside his body, empty... What was he doing? The hit-man from Chicago stopped; Massimo looked up. Then the strangest thing happened: Joe nodded towards the fat man and turned to look towards the far end of the room, towards the back door where Tommy stood. When his stunned gaze met Joe's eyes across the room, Tommy understood... His blood turned to ice as he suddenly realised what was happening. Gun in hand still, Tommy turned and started running, out of the back yard, past the old wooden gate, up the alley and on to the avenue.

As according to his perfect plan, the car was parked in front of the alley next to the café. But Tommy quickly realised he wouldn't have time to get in and drive away before Joe and Massimo's boy came out. Sure enough, he saw the café doors start to open. Before he turned left and fled, Tommy just about glimpsed Angelo's head leaning against the glass window, his dead eyes staring into space.

His legs were too old for it, and his coat was making him even heavier than his 220-odd pounds, but the hit-man knew well enough that his one and only chance was in a shameless flight. And as anywhere else in the world, the sight of a running man holding a gun made passers-by scream and scatter. Tommy pocketed his gun, keeping his hand on it, and ran on. A quick glance back; Massimo's bodyguard was running, pushing his way towards him; Joe was just standing in front of the café near one of the tall potted plants, watching.

His throat on fire, his legs about to give up, Tommy hooked a left turn off the avenue. He knew he couldn't run for too long like that. He turned and looked: the bodyguard with his shades was coming around the corner, still after him. Tommy, feeling he would drop if he tried to run any more, decided to turn around and stand his ground. His brain empty, he drew the gun out of his pocket. Might as well go down in an old-time shoot-out, he told himself. His pursuer saw him stop and slowed down, started walking towards him. Destiny was now thirty yards away, twenty yards...

Then the weirdest thing happened in an already weird evening: suddenly a dark van appeared around the corner, right in the middle of the road. Massimo's man, startled by the roar of the engine, was about to turn around just as the van levelled on him. Tommy watched in shock through the drops of sweat gathered around his eyes as an arm appeared out of the sliding door of the van and hit the bodyguard from the back as it came level. The man dropped his gun and fell flat on his face in the middle of the road. Then, as in a wild dream, the van came to an abrupt stop right by him. Within a few seconds, Tommy's gun was wrenched from his hand, then two strong arms grabbed his coat, dragged him off the ground and pulled him inside the van. He just about had time to hear the screaming of tyres as the van drove off and the slamming of the door behind him before something crashed on his skull and the lights went out.

They say out of the frying pan into the fire... Tommy was all but cooked already, or fried rather. With big Ws burned into his chest, thighs and buttocks, the fat hit-man looked like a grotesque swollen puppet. Just like his late colleague Paulie, he had finished hanging from a butcher's hook in Ice's friendless dance-hall. Tonight there was no music, though, and no guests other than him. Tommy's last dance was starting to turn into a grill party.

'I thought them mob guys were tougher than that!'

Booker dropped the poker and went to sit on an empty crate. Under the torture of the hot metal applied to his flesh, Tommy had passed out, for the second time.

'Wake his ass up; I ain't got all night,' Ice told him drily.

They had been interrogating Tommy for almost an hour. Early, just like with Paulie, hadn't said a word. He just leaned by the van, listening to the answers to Ice's questions, while Booker kept motivating the victim. Just like Paulie, Tommy had played hard at first, threatening his captors just like any self-respecting Italian wiseguy would do. But he quickly realised how desperate his situation was when Ice coldly explained who they were and what they wanted from him.

'If he gets a heart attack before he talks, we got nothing,' Booker told him calmly, then pushed two sticks of gum into his mouth.

'What? A heart attack?'

159

Booker explained, chewing all the while:

'When you're hanging on like that, your chest muscles contract and your lungs don't get enough air. After a while you have problems breathing. That guy's about two hundred and fifty pounds, too heavy to stand it much longer.'

Ice couldn't believe it. He had never heard Booker talk so much.

'You sound like a doctor. Where d'you learn all that?'

Booker didn't answer, just smoothed his low beard with one huge hand and kept on chewing.

Early regarded Ice for a few seconds, looking sombre.

'Maybe he's telling the truth.'

'No, man! His friend said he took the bag, remember?'

Ice went behind the bar, picked up a bottle of beer from the fridge. He motioned to Early but Early declined. Twist and open, one deep swallow. Ice shook his head.

'That fat motherfucker's trying to fuck us up. Like he's gonna be around to spend that money!'

Early wasn't so sure.

'He ain't that tough. He's about fifty, fat, at the end of his time. He's soft; if he had the money I think he would have talked.'

'So you buy that story about Lisa working for the cops?' Ice asked.

Early didn't answer right away. He would have like to have said he didn't, but the whole story was so shady that he was trying to keep an open mind to piece it all together. The only thing he was certain of was that Lisa had been shot by Tommy on Sal's order. The hit-man had admitted to that at least. But he stubbornly denied knowing anything about the missing money. So where did this police thing come from?

He signalled to Booker. 'Get him down, put him on the chair.'

Impassive, the big man got up and lifted Tommy off the hook, dropped him on one of the plastic bucket chairs. Handcuffed, naked, his diminutive manhood disappearing under the overhanging white flesh of his bloated stomach, he didn't look like much.

'Wake him up,' Early said.

Booker went to pick up the grey metal bucket he had already used once. Careful not to wet his expensive sweater, he flung the water on the sleeping Tommy. The white man only shook and snorted, but two firm slaps helped to get him fully awake.

'OK, Tommy boy; let's see if we get the story right ... and try not to fall asleep this time.' Ice came up, his beer bottle in hand.

With regained consciousness the pain from the burns came back. Tommy opened puffed-up eyes and realised the hopeless-ness of his situation. He muttered through

161

cracked lips:

'No more...'

'It ain't over till it's over, man,' Ice told him, then poured some of his beer over Tommy's mouth. 'Have a drink. You see: we ain't monsters.'

'You fucking molyan!' Tommy spluttered.

'He called you a molyan,' Booker pointed out.

Ice shrugged.

'I got to say, you're a brave man, you guinea cocksucker! Allright, we'll deal with that later. Now... You said two girls came to visit Sal at the club, right? Then one of them came back with a guy. She told Sal he was a cop and wanted her to set him up. She was wired, right?'

Tommy didn't answer. Booker stared at him, then glanced at the poker lying on the floor, cold by now. But that alone motivated the victim.

'Yeah... Right.'

'So you guys pulled up the guy and smoked him. Then Sal told you to take the girl out so she couldn't talk about it. Right?'

Tommy nodded, his face a mask of fear and hatred.

'Then you shot her and you took her money...'

This time Tommy reacted spontaneously:

'I didn't take no fucking money!'

'You took her bag. Your friend told us you

took it home with you.'

'I'm telling you there was no fucking money inside, all right?'

'What d'you do with the bag?'

'I burned it.'

'With all the stuff inside?'

'Yeah, I burned everything.'

Ice looked at Tommy straight for a moment, then turned to Early, listening from his corner. Early seemed to be lost in a reflection of his own for a while. The silence in the big warehouse was almost oppressive.

Finally, Early moved, walked up slowly to come and stop a few feet away from the fat naked man squeezed in the plastic chair. With his handsome dark brown face, inexpressive eyes, elegantly clothed in an expensive dark blue suit and tan shirt, Early appeared to Tommy as what he was: a young, cold and clear-headed businessman, a leader of men for whom emotions didn't exist in his line of work. At this hour, his last hour, the mob old-timer realised Sal had sadly slipped up. Then Early spoke and Tommy felt like the young black man had simply read his thoughts.

'My sister had a choice, and she saved your boss instead of giving him up to the cops. And you really think she would have sold him out after that?'

Tommy was finding it hard to stand Early's stare.

163

'Tell me about the other girl,' Early said.

Tommy swallowed painfully, mumbled:

'She was small with dark hair, dark eyes, like a ... a Latina or something.'

A pause, then Early asked:

'No name?'

'I don't know ... Sal didn't say...'

Early waited a little, then nodded slowly before turning away and walking back to his spot near the van. There and then Tommy felt his heart sink within his tortured chest.

'It was Sal's order...' he said, addressing the young black man, who wasn't looking at him any more.

A swift, silent eye movement from Early, a subtle facial expression barely lasting a second; he had given Booker his own order.

'We understand, Tommy. And don't worry; Sal'll be there with you real soon,' Ice said.

Tommy heard but didn't look his way. His eyes followed the big bearded executioner as he went to the van and returned with the black gun with the long barrel, his own gun. Between the two predators, in a stare that lasted several seconds, floated the call of death, the call of blood between victor and vanquished. The sagging of Tommy's naked, weary shoulders told his acceptance of the fate he had dealt to others so many times for so many years. Then the whole world shrank to become the small black hole at the end of the silencer.

'Do it ... I'm ready,' he said, a silent prayer to his favourite saint already on his lips.

Then he heard the voice, calm, composed, without a hint of anger.

'You shot my sister seven times, twice in the head ... but she survived.'

Tommy reopened his eyes, focusing on Early, who simply added:

'Let's see if you're as tough as her.'

Then the gun went 'plop' and the first bullet hit him in the left knee. Tommy screamed.

Ice shook his head disapprovingly.

'Try to die with a little dignity, wiseguy.'

The old joke that FBI guys sleep with their pants on was probably true after all, Burrows reflected as he stepped out of his car. Seven a.m. Sunday morning, ten minutes' drive from his house, and the two agents were already on the scene before him, as sharply dressed as ever...

'Where d'you guys live?' he quipped, nodding to the young uniform who lifted the tape for him to enter the already cordoned-off perimeter.

'Just as well you didn't have time for breakfast,' Bronski said as a greeting, nodding towards the door of the restaurant.

Burrows could see Carter's head amongst a dozen cops, most of them uniforms, except for his own precinct colleague, Rhonda. He walked towards them, answered a few salutes, wishing he had left town for the weekend to go fishing as he had originally planned.

'What we got, Rhonda?' he asked the short and stout black officer, looking like a tourist in her green jogging suit and headband.

'Morning, Louis. Nothing too pretty.'

The shape was covered with a grey tarpaulin sheet. Burrows lifted a corner and winced; nothing pretty, Rhonda was right about that. The man seated against the restaurant door had had a really bad Saturday night, his last in fact. Dressed only in striped shorts, his overweight pale body rested in its final pose like a beached whale on the sand. The dead man was a dreadful sight. The dried bloodstains all over, with dark red tracks running down to the ground, testified to a slow and painful death. One end of the black nylon rope tied around the neck of the corpse was fastened to the door handle of the restaurant like a dog leash. Burrows dropped the corner of the sheet.

'What's with the W marks?' he asked.

'Burns. Looks like a cattle prod to me,' Carter answered from behind him. But for his Brooklyn accent, the tall blond agent could easily have passed for a Texan ranch hand.

'Tortured, eh?' Burrows remarked.

'You know the customer?' Bronski enquired.

'Oh, yeah; Tommy Dilario, Sal Scaffone's head gorilla. An old-timer, tough as nails,' Burrows said, frowning.

He could remember pulling in Tommy almost ten years earlier, for a homicide. He knew he was guilty, but had to let him go the very next day: no gun, no evidence.

'Someone threw a hot party last night,' Bronski commented, deadpan. 'Seen enough?'

Burrows made a face that said he had.

'Then come on; I'm buying you breakfast.'

'OK.' Burrows accepted the offer.

It was Sunday, after all, and he deserved at least one real breakfast a week.

'Rhonda?' he called out to his colleague, who was talking to one of the print men to the side.

'Tomorrow, Louis. Have a nice day.' She waved to him.

Burrows got back to his car and followed the two men.

'What we got here, Detective?'

They had settled at the last table of the diner, where they couldn't be overheard. Apart from a young long-haired couple in bike leather and two black kids stuffing pancakes at the front, the place was quiet.

167

The sun was rising in an almost blue sky, but passers-by in their anoraks showed no one trusted the early spring promise just yet.

'I was hoping you could tell me,' Burrows answered Bronski between two bites of his scrambled egg.

The FBI veteran was on black coffee, an untouched doughnut on a plate in front of him, while Carter the blond giant worked hard at munching on a long salad-and-something French bread sandwich.

'The word on the street is that Sal is having a war with Fat Massimo from Queens.'

Bronski was waiting on Burrows' reaction, but the seasoned cop simply shrugged and picked up a fried tomato with his fork.

'Sal's lost two men in two days; he's losing,' he said.

'Only I don't buy that line.'

'You don't?'

Carter wiped some mayonnaise from his mouth and agreed.

'We don't. You're from here, Burrows, you know the score with mob guys; when was the last time you heard of a turf war between them in New York?'

'About fifteen years.'

'Right. So why would they call attention to themselves now? That's not how they do things any more. They get together, get a mediator and work things out.'

Burrows thought about it, made a face that said he wasn't sure.

'It's not old man Scaffone calling the shots any more. Maybe Sal is too hot blooded and can't handle disputes. You checked on Fat Massimo's side, I guess...'

Bronski nodded.

'We sure did. There was an incident yesterday around his place. Difficult to get witnesses down there, it's an Italian neighbourhood, but something happened. Tommy might have been seen in the area...'

'So it was that: he went down there to talk it out and they took him out,' Burrows said, though he didn't sound as convinced as he wanted to.

Carter stretched, his stomach now filled. He signalled to the young woman behind the counter, raising his empty coffee cup, then told Burrows:

'Could be, but there's more; besides Sal's driver, delivered to him dead yesterday, two more of his men might be missing.'

'How d'you know that?'

'Inside info.' Carter smiled at the waitress pouring him more coffee, waited until she'd left. 'We got reliable sources inside, but there's something real strange going on; nobody can confirm that Massimo started all this. He's a businessman now, wouldn't do him no good to kick up a war.'

Burrows finished his breakfast. The strong

black coffee had cleared his mind. He looked at Bronski, sipping some more of the stuff.

'So, bodies are turning up on Sal's doorstep but you don't believe the obvious. Why don't you tell me what's on your mind.'

He waited for the FBI man to speak up.

'Did you read the report on Sal's driver?' Bronski asked.

'Not yet.'

'His body had the same burn marks you saw on Tommy this morning.'

Burrows waited for more, looked at Carter, who nodded but said nothing.

'So both guys were tortured...'

'Right.' Bronski let a few seconds pass, then asked: 'Why?'

'Why?' Burrows repeated, trying to see where it was going.

'Yeah: why? This is not the way mob guys work. They kill and make you disappear, or kill and send the body as a message, but torture is not common with them.'

'Meaning?'

'Meaning ... maybe we're reading this all wrong,' Carter completed.

Burrows knew the two agents had a theory on this, and they wanted him to get there too. He said:

'OK, so you don't think it's what it looks like. But if Massimo didn't hit Sal ... who did?'

Carter and Bronski exchanged a look, like they were smarter than him or something. It made Burrows frustrated.

'OK, you guys are the smartest, as always. Just spare me the gloating and tell me what you got.'

'We got nothing,' Carter told him. 'Nothing but suspicions.'

Then Bronski asked:

'Got anything on your missing girl?'

Burrows looked at him, frowned and shook his head.

'Nothing. Why?'

'Why? 'Cause I got a crazy idea, but it's a crazy world and I'd like you to tell me what you think about that...'

Bronski paused, making sure he had Burrows' full attention.

'The story so far: an undercover DEA agent tries to set up Sal. There's a girl in the picture but we don't know for sure who she's playing with. The DEA man disappears, the next day we find the girl shot, left for dead. Next thing we know, she walks out of intensive care and disappears too. A couple of days later, Sal's men start to turn up dead, tortured and delivered to him...'

Bronski waited, then asked:

'You with me?'

'I'm starting to be,' Burrows answered.

In his mind, he was busy connecting the loose ends; Bronski's theory sounded very

171

interesting all of a sudden.

'So you're saying the girl was part of the set-up?'

Bronski made a gesture that said he didn't know for sure.

'She was right in the middle of it. I'd be real surprised if it was a coincidence.'

Something was bothering Burrows.

'Tell me about this DEA surveillance... You said the undercover agent was talking to the girl when they lost contact, right?'

'Yeah. One minute, their guy's talking to this girl, then the line goes dead.'

'What about?'

'What?'

'What were they talking about?' Burrows asked.

'I don't know...'

'You didn't listen to the tape?'

'We tried to, but the DEA people ain't very cooperative. You know how things are between agencies...'

'You talked to the other agent?' Burrows asked.

'We've been trying to, but the guy's gone missing.'

There was a pause. Both men locked eyes for a few seconds and realised they were thinking alike. It was Burrows who said it:

'Something's funny here: we got to find that agent and talk to him.'

More people were now arriving in the

diner, men with their kids in tow, couples. The place was getting more noisy. Burrows said:

'So, if you got things right, the girl's people are after Sal for revenge...'

Bronski smiled but it wasn't real smile.

'If she's Hanley's daughter and her family found out that Sal got her shot, then it all makes sense.'

That sounded worrying.

'If that's the case, I think they would have blown up Sal's place with him inside, something like that. Jamaicans usually go for maximum effect,' Burrows pointed out.

'Right,' Carter butted in. 'But we're not dealing with the average Jamaican here. If Sal is still alive, it means there's something more, something we don't know yet.'

'We don't want things to blow up between these guys and the mob in Brooklyn,' Burrows said. 'That's a nightmare scenario, we got to make sure it doesn't happen.'

Carter nodded. 'You got that right.'

Bronski looked absent for a moment, then he said:

'If who I think is behind this, Sal's in deep shit.'

On the couch, Booker was sleeping like a baby. After downing two platefuls of Mary-lee's Mexican chili con carne, the big enforcer had dropped into slumber while

173

trying to follow a ball game on the sports channel.

Patiently, Marylee coaxed Lisa to eat one more spoonful of the food. Despite the damage inflicted on her jaws, the convalescent girl was managing to chew now. She had to eat slowly, a little at a time, but she was eating. And getting back strength, Marylee could see it. Although Lisa still couldn't move her limbs, she looked better; her wounds were closing well, which was a good sign. Every day, Marylee bathed her, massaged her body with olive oil, fed her fruit juices and soups and talked to her. She believed talking to her would soothe Lisa's spirit, give her confidence and hope.

To Marylee, it was Lisa's spirit itself which would heal her. She was convinced the girl's paralysis was only temporary and caused by a nervous block rather than physiological damage. She told Ice that, although she had left her job at LA County Hospital after only a few months, her nursing training was proving useful. Just like so many other things that happened to her, the fact that she was able to tend to Lisa and help her survive her ordeal was God's will. That was the way she lived; seeing God's hands at work in many places.

Out in the garden, under the bamboo canopy covered over with climber vine plants, Ice and Early were sipping carrot juice. Brooklyn-born Ice had learned the subtleties of Jamaican cuisine from his Jamaican mother, and kept it up.

'So what you think happened to the money?' he asked his cousin.

Early had been spinning this same question in his mind since the previous night.

'I really don't know. Something missing in that story.'

'You think the hit-man was lying?'

'He was in a lot of pain, but even when Booker shot him in the knees, he kept saying he didn't know about the money. Unless...'

Ice waited for Early to speak his mind.

'Unless the guy gave his boss the money and didn't want us to know.'

Ice looked doubtful.

'You really believe the guy could be that tough?'

'He knew he was dead anyway, he could have done it just to fuck us up. Them mob guys can be very loyal, loyal unto death,' Early explained.

'His boss didn't know about the money. I can't see why the guy would give up some loot for no reason.'

'Yeah, it don't make no sense.' After a silent moment, Early asked: 'What you think about this cop story?'

'I don't know, man. I've been thinking about that. Let's say the guy was telling the truth; why would Lisa make up a story like

that? She must have been under pressure,'
Ice said.

'You mean the cops had something on her
and forced her to set up Sal?'

'I don't know, but it's the only way she
could have done it.'

'But Lisa didn't have no shit with her.
What could the cops want with her?'

Early was puzzled by that.

'I don't know, but if they wanted to set up
Sal, then sending Lisa was the best way to
play it.'

'Yeah, but Lisa gave up the cop and he got
fucked up.'

Ice smiled, shook his head.

'Lisa's one tough girl, no shit!'

'She's a Hanley, blood.'

'Right.' Ice nodded, then said: 'If the dead
cop sent Lisa down there, he must have had
something on her. But that also means she
knew Sal already. That's what I can't figure
out: how Lisa could know a mob guy like
Sal. What was she doing in that place?'

Early had already been spending most of
the night turning all these questions in his
mind.

'The other girl must have brought her to
the club. That's the only way.'

'Yeah, but who the fuck is that girl?'

Early asked his cousin:

'You know if Lisa have any friends in New
York? She ever mentioned somebody?'

'I asked Marylee already: nobody. When she comes over, she just stays at the apartment but she spends most of her time with Marylee.'

'The guy said the girl looked like a Latina...' Early reflected, talking to himself.

'You know Lisa: she don't trust nobody, Early, she wouldn't hang out with a Puerto Rican,' Ice pointed out.

'Yeah, you're right. But she went to a mob club with a girl, that's what I can't understand.'

They both thought about that enigma for a while, the timid sun playing across the intertwined branches of the climbing vine above them, drawing shadow patterns on their clothes. Then Ice said:

'You know something; we got to find out about that DEA operation.'

'How you gonna do that?'

Ice smiled.

'Out of all the cops, narcotics are the easiest ones to buy, the most greedy. They see too much money moving around... I got an idea. Let me make a few moves, I'll see what I can dig up.'

'All right. I feel that's where we can get some answers.'

Ice's mobile rang. He checked the number on the screen, answered.

'Yeah... You all right?... No, stand by... Yeah, I know, but you wait till I call you back... Cool ... I'm calling you back.'

Only a man who knew him as well as Early did could have detected it on his face, but when he hung up Ice was angry.

'What happen?'

'Just some little problems ... I'm sorting it out, don't worry.' Ice looked like he didn't really want to talk about the matter.

'Problems like what?'

'Just some heat...' Early's eyes were watching him, waiting. Ice went on:

'Well, you know we had to close down the house on Osbourne Street a couple of months ago... The cops were on to it. We set up another place but we're getting static from some guys. I had to step up security. They shot one of my runners two weeks ago, but we smoked two of them right after that. It's kinda tense right now.'

'So what's up?'

'It was Mickey O: the house got attacked this morning ... fire-bombed... They say it's the same guys.'

'Locals trying to muscle in on you?' Early sounded surprised.

Ice shook his head.

'No, local niggers wouldn't fuck around in Crown Heights. It's a bunch of youths from Yard who just moved earlier this year.'

'Jamaicans?' Early asked, intrigued.

'Yeah. I heard they landed in Jersey first but they got pushed out, so they're trying to

178

set up some runnings up here.'

'Who's supplying them?'

'Nobody I know. But they got quality stuff, and 'nough of it, it looks like.' Ice sounded frustrated. He added, 'But nobody's moving in on my patch. I've already arranged their send-off party.'

Early said nothing for a moment. He seemed to be thinking it over, then he said:

'I don't know if it's worth it, you know.'

'What d'you mean?'

'Dying and killing for a few blocks of concrete... It's never gonna end anyway.'

'What you talking about, man?'

More quiet reflection from Early, his gaze out the window, before he asked:

'Tell me something, Ice. You remember your father?'

It was Ice's turn to fall silent for a few seconds.

'Why you ask me that?'

'Just tell me.'

Ice sighed, shrugged.

'Mama used to take me down south to visit him a couple times a year, when he was doing time in Georgia. He was big ... he looked big to me at the time anyway. I was just a kid, just about seven or eight.'

'You spent time with him when he came out?'

'After he came out, I went down to where he lived, for the school vacation. Him and

179

my ma were done by then. I stayed with his mother, my grandma ... she was cool. He used to be out most of the time.'

Memories were sending Ice back in time, way back.

'He was too busy to spend time with you,' Early told his cousin. 'My father was like that too. The life he lived, he couldn't be a family man, he just didn't have the time.'

There was a pause as both seemed to be caught in reminiscing.

'You got a baby coming, Ice; you don't want to be live like that,' Early stated flatly.

Ice was thinking about that now. He glanced inside, towards the living room, where Marylee was still tending to Lisa. Then he looked at Early.

'So what you saying, man; you want to quit?'

A pause before Early answered.

'The business we're into ... it's just like boxing: you got to know when to hang up your gloves.'

Ice was listening, thinking about it.

'You ever see an old drug dealer?' Early asked him. He made a face. 'This drug business is a drug in itself, Ice. It can make poor kids like us grow up to own things we could never dream of. You fight your way up, but for every one that makes it, how many drop down along the way? You have to step over people to get there, that's the way it is.'

'It's survival. Either that or you end up begging, on the street or at the welfare office, but it's still begging,' Ice said.

Early nodded.

'Yeah, it's survival. Then you get to the top, you run things, you have money everywhere, and respect, everything that makes a man feel like he's somebody. But you can't trust no one, even your best friend can betray you, because there's just too much money in it, and that makes it deadly.'

Early paused, then added:

'But you can't live like that all your life. If you make it, you better know when to drop it.'

After a long silence Early finished speaking his mind:

'That's what my father's life, and his death, taught me.'

'So you want out of the game, right?' Ice asked, still finding it hard to believe.

Early sighed.

'Sometimes, you get signs in life, like ... messages. And when you get signs like that, you better watch out. You see what happened to Lisa ... I see it as a sign.'

Ice was listening, thinking about what Early meant.

'You think it's a warning, eh?'

'Yeah. You know what was the last thing my father told me on the phone?... Look after Lisa; that.' Early shook his head. 'And

181

look what I got her into, look at her!'

'Don't blame it all on yourself, man; shit happens,' Ice said, trying to ease up the guilt he could see his cousin felt.

'Shit like that isn't supposed to happen to her, Ice. She's wasn't supposed to get involved in the business, the old man didn't want that for her, for none of us He wanted us to make money in straight-up, legal business. He worked hard, risked his life and his freedom for years, just so we wouldn't have to live that way, the way he lived.'

Early had been thinking hard about all that for a long time, since his father's death two years before in fact. The state of Lisa when he saw her on arriving in New York a couple of days earlier had been a shock to him, a stern and soul-chilling reminder of his father's last will. He told Ice:

'Check it out; right now I don't need to run drugs no more to make a living. With the businesses the old man set up, I make more than enough to live good. I run my club, money ain't short. I phased out of the runnings back in Miami, I get less problems. Now it looks like things getting tight up here, maybe we should let it go altogether.'

Ice finished his juice. He felt as weary as Early of fighting turf wars all the time. The killings, the cops, the constant stress of having to defend your operations from a crowd of hungry enemies. But how else could it be, when so much was at stake?

'I know what you're saying, man; I feel that way too sometimes. And Marylee's been bugging me to leave the game behind. If I listened to her, we'd just move to the West Coast, open a couple shops and a restaurant or something!'

Ice smiled, thinking about his wife's dearest wishes.

'But I have a lot of people working for me, they got families to feed too...'

He paused, looking sombre.

'It's deadly on the street, you know how things work out there. When you're on top of the heap, those below you won't let you go back down; they'll eat you first.'

Early looked at him, didn't say a word.

Aldo the chef had done it just right. It was Giuseppe Scaffone's favourite meal, and although he had prepared it a thousand times for his old boss, it wasn't often now-adays that he got to do so. And Don Scaffone had enjoyed it to the full, Aldo was sure of it. But it didn't show.

Right now, the old man was slowly sipping his glass of wine from the old country with a stern look set across his brow. Matty had eaten little, while Sal had hardly touched his plate. Lunch in the closed restaurant had been a quiet affair. Neither Matty nor Sal wanted to talk first, each for his own reasons. Don Scaffone didn't come to Brooklyn without a good reason these days, so when Pete, his 'secretary', had called the previous evening to inform Sal he would be coming for Sunday lunch, his nervous nephew had received the news like the announcement of the last supper. And it felt like that now. Aldo came over.

'Did you enjoy it, Don Scaffone?' he asked, eyes watching the old man's face for signs.

'Molto bene, eccellente, amico mio.'

Aldo smiled and nodded. Reassured that Don Scaffone's serious countenance had nothing to do with his cooking, he started clearing the table.

Matty took out a cigarette, lit it. Sal was too tense to do so right now, though he badly felt the need for a puff of tobacco. Like he had read his mind, the old man said:

'You can smoke if you want, Sal.'

That definitely made Sal feel even worse. His uncle's affable tone made it sound like the traditional offer of the last cigarette to a condemned man. He took out his pack.

'So, who's going to talk to me first?'

Don Scaffone had already had all the information, Sal and Matty both knew that, but he needed to hear it all from the parties concerned. Sal wasn't going to be stupid enough to let Matty talk; that would be the final nail for him. He was a man and expected to justify his actions as a man; that was the way his uncle had brought him up.

'OK, I have a few problems...' he started, then cleared his throat which suddenly felt rather dry. 'I ... I was going to come and tell you about it ... but I wanted to sort things out myself first.'

Sal's feeble attempt at an excuse was received as it deserved to be by his uncle.

'But you didn't sort it out, did you, Sal?'

There was no menace in the old man's tone, none at all, but Sal's blood was going colder by the minute. He knew how serious the situation was, and he knew it was all down to his going against his uncle's express will.

'No,' he answered meekly.

Matty pulled on his cigarette, screened by the smoke, keeping as still as he could. His turn to be asked questions would come, he knew.

'Tell me about your problems, Sal,' Don Scaffone said, sounding almost like a psychoanalyst.

Sal waited a few seconds, then started:

'The cops have been watching me. They been watching the place for some time ... a couple of months, like. I noticed because they started having these vans parked across the street, unmarked cars always hanging

185

around watching the restaurant, things you notice, you know... Then some guys always coming in, like customers ... they come in and they eat, drink and everything... But I see them watching, watching who's there, watching me. I didn't know what they wanted so one time I came up to one of them, I ask them why they were doing this, you know, coming in and watching my business all the time. They said they didn't know what I was talking about. I knew they were cops, and they knew I knew, but they said they liked my place and nobody said cops couldn't come in and eat. They said they loved the food! Imagine that!'

Whether Don Scaffone could imagine or not, he didn't say, simply nodded, so Sal went on:

'So anyway, one night, last week ... no, weekend before last, these guys, DEA cops, they burst in with guns and dogs and all that ... they raided the place... The place is full and suddenly there's cops and dogs everywhere, they're shoving people around, turning the place upside down and everything. I was upstairs in the office, so I come down to see what's all the noise ... they stick me up, cuffed me right away ... in front of the customers and everybody, like I'm some criminal or something. They searched the whole place, took away my files. Next thing I know they dragging me to the precinct in the middle of the night, just like that!'

Sal paused, as if the memories of that terrible evening were too stressful to even talk about.

'So I'm down in this place with four or five cops asking me questions. They said like they had some cop in my place, like a ... an undercover ... and they lost him. So I said, "So? What's that go to do with me?" It's like they sent a guy to my place to spy on me or something, then the guy disappears or something, I don't know ... then they're accusing me! I told them I didn't know about their friend and I wanted to call my lawyer. They had me in there for two hours before I got a call out! Some crazy story...'

Don Scaffone was listening to the crazy story. As Sal stopped, he asked:

'That's all?'

Sal made a face.

'That's what happened ... but after that, when the lawyer was there, they had to explain what they wanted with me, why they busted in on me like that, without a warrant! They said, like, they're DEA and they been watching the place. They said they're look-ing for drugs. Drugs, in my place! I told them they were making a mistake; we don't do drugs, we leave it to niggers and spics ... I told them they got the wrong information.'

After a few seconds thinking all this over, the old man turned to Matty.

'You was going to tell me all this, Matty...'

It wasn't so much a question as a statement of fact, meaning Matty should have done so already.

'Yeah, but we've had all this trouble happening at the same time...' Matty looked embarrassed, though only Don Scaffone could tell.

'Trouble, yeah... That's what I came to talk to you about, Sal.'

Sal waited, knowing it was always best to find out first what the old man knew already.

'How many men have you lost?'

Sal sighed deeply, like the question brought up sorrow.

'Tommy, Paulie, Angelo ... Joe.'

The old man's face was hard, eyes focused behind the tired, wrinkled eyelids. 'I've had to call your Aunt Sophia to tell her about Angelo.'

Sal had a fleeting thought for an old, overweight woman who might not just survive the death of her youngest son. Then he heard the old man ask him something that threw him:

'Sal, who brought Joe to you?'

'Joe?... Tommy brought him in. He had to leave Chicago after the Shark was killed...'

'But you never checked out his cards yourself.'

Bewildered, Sal looked at Matty, who

188

looked at Don Scaffone in surprise.

'Joe was on the run. Tommy knew him from years before when they worked in Chicago together on the docks.'

Don Scaffone coughed, shook his head.

'And Joe told Tommy he had to run because the Shark's killer was after him, right?'

Sal looked at Matty, who said:

'Right.'

'You used to be sharper than that, Matty. You're like me; you're getting old.'

The remark sounded mild, but Matty knew his old boss too well not to feel the sting in his guts. Neither he nor Sal said a word, waiting for the bad news.

'Joe was paid to set up the Shark. He ran because the killers decided he had to go too.'

Silence followed the awful revelation from the old man. How did he get to know that? Don Scaffone explained in his quiet old-country voice:

'Joe came to Tommy because he knew no one could touch him if he worked for us. And no one would talk either, else they would sell themselves out; the Shark had lots of friends.'

Sal said:

'Joe's dead now, he paid for his treason.'

A faint smile seemed to lighten the old man's countenance for a short few seconds.

Then he asked:

'Did they send back his body to you?' Sal frowned.

'No, but he didn't make it back...'

'But you got Paulie, Tommy and Angelo's bodies...?'

'Yeah...'

Don Scaffone took time to sip from the wineglass he had hardly touched, swallowed slowly like aged men do, before speaking:

'I got bad news for you, Sal: Joe is alive and well. He lives above Massimo's place.'

A dozen saints straight from heaven crashing through the roof of the restaurant couldn't have stunned Sal any more than the words from his uncle.

'What?' Matty said, just as shocked.

'If a man betrays once and stays alive, he will betray again,' Don Scaffone stated calmly. Then he asked:

'What started the problems between you and Massimo?'

Sal was feeling worse by the minute now.

'Massimo's been watching us for some time, he wants to move in on us. He waited until you retired to try his luck.'

'Maybe I shouldn't have retired,' the old man said, and both Matty and Sal knew what that meant; Sal wasn't ready to lead the family and Matty hadn't done his job of advising Sal properly.

'So Massimo and you don't have any

personal problems, right? It's just him want-ing to expand his business?'

Sal didn't answer. He had just realised that, somehow, his uncle knew. He was right.

'I got to tell you something, *figlio mio*: you can take a man's table, his chair, his clothes and his shoes even; if you give them back, he might forgive you. But if you take his bed and use his sheet, you can never make it up to him.'

A heavy silence followed the old man's words. Sal was looking somewhere on the far wall, while Matty was concentrating on the tablecloth. Then Don Scaffone switched to what he really wanted to know:

'So, Matty, what can you tell me about this police thing, the drugs guys ... what you call them?'

'DEA,' Matty answered sombrely.

'Yeah, the DEA... What's this all about?'

Matty was treading a fine line and he knew it. Deep inside he cursed himself for not obeying his first instinct and tipping his boss about Sal when it all first began. He tried to steer a safe course.

'They came down and raided the place, last week. They said they been watching us. Looks like some people been trying to set us up.'

'They find anything?'

'No, nothing.'

'But they said somebody been involved with drugs, one of us, right?'

'Yeah, that's what they said.'

Don Scaffone nodded slowly, then asked Sal:

'You have any ideas?' Sal almost had a heart attack right there and then; his stomach tightened. But then the old man asked again:

'You noticed any of your guys acting funny, suspicious, like? Maybe having more money to spend than what you're paying him...?'

For Sal this came like a life-raft to a sinking man. He grabbed it.

'I don't know. I can't be sure but you could be right... A couple of times I noticed like someone was flashing a little too much cash, you know; new car, nice clothes, spending on broads more than he used to.'

'You see, you can always tell if you look carefully. Who is it?'

Sal made a face like he felt bad fingering the man.

'Like I said, I got no proof, but the guy's been spreading money around a little.'

Don Scaffone waited. He wouldn't ask the question twice, Sal knew that. He made a gesture of apology.

'I feel bad to accuse him, but ... it's Paulie, may his soul rest in peace.'

Matty and Sal's eyes locked for a fraction

of a second. Then Matty looked slowly around the room, like he expected Paulie's ghost to come down sword in hand on Sal to avenge the slander.

Don Scaffone sighed, shook his head in disappointment.

'He was a nice kid, but it happens a lot nowadays. It's hard to keep your people from getting involved in this thing. Too much money...'

'Sorry, I should have seen it earlier,' Sal said, sounding genuinely contrite.

'It's not your fault, you can't watch everybody all the time. It could happen to anybody.'

Matty, feeling the weight of the old man's gaze on him, glanced his way: right there and then he knew the man who would fool Don Scaffone was yet to be born.

The dark and sullen-looking youth sat watching the TV but not seeing it, that was clear. Ice, on the phone to someone, knew him well enough to realise his young lieu-tenant was just about to get drastic. Mickey O had been in the crack house earlier that day when it got fire-bombed. He knew where it came from and was for immediate and final action; but he knew Early wouldn't have liked any brash talking.

'Right ... yeah ... I know ... no, you wait till I call you ... yeah, you wait ... I call you back at nine, for real ... all right ... yeah ... nine o'clock, man ... cool.'

Ice cut off the call.

'All right, everybody off the block for now, too much police around.'

O looked at him, asked:

'What about the boyz dem?'

'Hold it down.'

'Hol' it down? I was inside when fire broke out at three o'clock this morning, you know, Ice! Me and Picka, and about twenty customers. Tho' we know how dem operate and we put up a glass 'pon the slot, the bwai dem set fire to the whole floor in front of the steel door. Hell to get out, man. De bwai dem try burn me up; me nah play no more, you see me?'

Ice nodded, understanding, and feeling the same way.

'I know how you feel, O ... but you stand by, fe now.'

The look across the dark handsome features was pure frustration.

'Ice, yuh ah hear me, time not playing for us right now, by tonight, dem plan fe shoot we off the street and start selling 'pon we fe block! Everybody watching: if we don't deal with them now, we out.'

Ice glanced at Early, his silent self as always, listening, analysing. Booker seemed totally absorbed in the cop series on the box, once in a while sipping from a large plastic jug of iced yogurt.

Ice sighed.

'O, you know me, I don't mek a bwai diss me and run ... but hold ev'rything down till tonight, all right? Just keep your teams out of sight and ready. I call you at eight-thirty, just wait for your orders.'

Straight faced, O listened, kept the same mask for a few more seconds after Ice stopped talking. Over six feet, broad shouldered with fine features and well-cropped hair, O could have aspired to be a model, something like Tyson Beckford maybe, but he was the nineteen-year-old trusted lieutenant of one of the largest drug operators in Brooklyn and ruled his territory with an iron hand.

He got up.

'All right, eight-thirty. I keep the man dem cool till that time.'

Ice looked at him and nodded; they both understood each other.

'Don, respeck. Later still.'

Early touched the offered fist, stood the youth's gaze. He might have seen him around the old area when he used to spend time in Jamaica. A short five years before, O would have been just a brash street teenager. Not any more.

'Yes, soldier.'

O was gone. Booker didn't even seem like he noticed.

'You see what I'm talking about?' Ice drank some of the beer he had hardly touched. 'We got hit twice in three weeks. If we don't deal with them right now, it's all over.'

'You're right,' Early said.

'Right. I'm right and I'm gonna do what is right, but the right way.'

Early said:

'Everything is happening at the same time.'

Ice was scratching his chin, looking absorbed.

'Yeah.' He got up. 'I'm gonna get the information you need ... about the DEA cop. Then I get a shower and we move out.' He left the room. Early asked:

'Hey, Booker, I feel like I know that youth, the one who just left.'

Booker's eyes hardly left the TV, just long enough to acknowledge Early's question.

'Dem used to call him Deacon. Him is Alvin little brother, from over Denham town.'

'Hmm,' Early said, remembering Alvin, one of his father's earliest and best soldiers back then.

They left the house together around 7.30. Ice drove in silence but for the background of a local radio show kicking sounds through the Tannoys. They got to the river, drove along a quiet backstreet to a quay. From where they parked, the lights of the monster city of Manhattan sparked the darkish blue sky across Brooklyn Bridge.

'Forty-five, he'll be there soon. He never comes first,' Ice explained.

Early had been even more quiet than usual; he had found out who had shot his sister but wasn't anywhere near getting back his money, with three days to go to the Colombian deadline.

'He's here,' Ice said, as a car passed by the van before coming to a stop fifty yards farther along the quay. Ice opened his door.

'Five minutes.' He left and walked slowly to the car, all the while checking around, just out of habit.

The man at the wheel was heavy set, black of hair and moustache, with a brown leather jacket over a purple designer T-shirt.

'Franco!' Ice said as he sank in the leather. The engine was gently purring, the car smelling of Kentucky fried chicken.

'Hey, Ice, how you doing?'

The smile was fat yet lacking warmth.

'Not as good as you, man.'

'Yeah ... yeah; I heard you had little problems lately.'

Ice nodded.

'Yeah, lately...' he repeated.

'You need help keeping things under control? 'Cause you know you got to keep things down.'

'I didn't call you to hear you talking smart to me, all right?' Ice cut the man sharply.

'OK ... OK, man; don't get angry. I'm just saying; I'm here to help, just in case, you know...'

Ice didn't return the false smile.

'What d'you know about an operation on Sal?'

'Sal?'

'Sal, yeah, Big Sal ... he's supposed to have a lot of your friends after him? What's the story?'

For the first time, Franco dropped his smirking look.

'The story? You want the story?... Don't go and eat there, go to McDonald's: it's better for your health.'

Ice stared at the man. He'd never quite taken to the sleazy-looking cop. The damn man was always so cheerfully devious and carefree looking! But they had a working relationship which helped their respective jobs. This time it was a big favour Ice needed. Sure enough, Franco felt it: he was fat but not quite dumb.

'You looking like you already been there to eat, like you got stomach ache,' he said, shaking his head.

'Franco, I need some information, need it bad. What d'you know about a DEA covert operation on Sal?'

Franco pouted like he usually did when he thought he held the upper hand.

'I only know they're interested in him. Apparently they have a man in his walls.'

'Yeah? You know the agents who run this?'

'I'm down at the 6-7, Ice, not at DEA!'

'But you could find out, right?'

Ice sounded pressing, uptight.

Franco seemed to shrivel a little, stopped his beaming.

'What's up with you, Ice, man, you usually cool.'

Ice sighed, faced the man square.

'Look, Franco, I'm having a rough week; all right? Business problems, family problems ... I'm sorting out everything at the same time, so I'm a little tense, you know what I'm saying?'

Franco knew.

'Yeah, I get like that too sometimes. You know what it's like when you wake up in the morning and you know you gonna have a bad day? You don't know why exactly but you just know. It ever happened to you?'

'Yeah, this morning.' Ice smiled but Franco could see it wasn't meant as a smile. 'In fact it happened to me every day this week, man. So right now, it's Sunday night and I would really love to have a better week, you see what I mean, Franco?'

Franco nodded, looking concerned.

'Yeah, man, I know what you mean.'

'OK, so, this what I know: Sal's been doing deals, powder deals, all right, and the DEA got a team on him. But something went wrong, one of their agents disappeared inside Sal's place, they just lost him. And so far they got nothing on him.'

Franco listened, his sharp, dark little eyes focused.

'So?'

'So, Sal ordered a hit on a young woman who was with the DEA guy when he disappeared... She's family.'

'Oh, shit!' Franco exclaimed, his face serious now.

'Yeah, shit. You hear anything about that, Franco?'

Franco didn't answer right away, looking like he was thinking it over for a little while. When he looked into Ice's face, his eyes had shrunk some more.

'Sal's having a rough time on the other side, too, now that you mention it. His people being sent back to him stiff, I heard.'

'Sal's mob disputes is not my concern,' Ice said. 'What I need to know is about the DEA cops. What can you do for me?'

'What you need?' Franco asked.

'What do I need? There was two guys on the surveillance team last week. I need the name of the one that's still alive ... and I need to know where I can find him.'

Franco listened; blew air between his

chubby lips.

'It's not gonna be easy. DEA's a closed shop for poor precinct cops like me. I don't cross no lines, man.'

Ice's eyes locked onto Franco's puffy sockets.

'I need this info, and I need it tonight,' he stated firmly.

'Tonight?' Franco's eyes widened just a little.

'Tonight, Franco.' Ice paused, his face set hard, just looking straight at the cop. He added: 'It's worth a lot to me.'

Franco sighed, nodded like he felt Ice's need.

'OK, OK, Ice, if it's worth that much to you ... I'm gonna try, give me a couple of hours, all right?'

'All right. I knew I could count on you, man.'

'Sure, Ice, but you know I'm sticking my neck out for you here. If anybody at DEA even dreams I'm sniffing around their garden, I'm in deep shit!'

'I know. Do your best, Franco: I won't forget it.'

'OK.'

Ice nodded and clicked the door open.

'I call you around ten.'

'Ten-thirty,' Franco corrected.

'OK, later.'

Ice closed the door and walked back to his

van. Franco's car effected a quick U-turn and drove away.

Early waited until Ice had kicked up the engine.

'I'll get something in a couple of hours.'

Ice shifted into gear, turned and moved out. Picking up his phone, he told Early:

'Now, play number two.'

He dialled O's number.

Ice steered the van around the corner of the block, parked a little way before the entrance to the brightly lit deli. A half-dozen teenagers, boys and girls, were loudly chatting on the sidewalk, the beats from one of the parked car's stereos pumping out, blending with their heckling and laughter.

'O be here soon... Looks like they waiting for something.' Ice motioned to the patrol car parked a couple of hundred yards up the street.

Two men, both tall and lean, came by the van window, trying to get Ice's attention. With a flick of the finger, he lowered his window.

'Hey, what's up, home?' Baseball cap low over his eyes, extra-large Fubu sweater on, the youth was bobbing on the spot.

'Cool,' Ice answered soberly.

'What's up, Ice, man, we been looking for you...'

Ice's cold stare cut the other man out.

'Looking for me?'

'Yeah, I mean, we glad to see you, man!' With beady eyes, the man had a slightly comical grin that seemed etched permanently across his face.

'What's your problem?' Ice asked the man, who was now getting as jittery as his friend. The first one came to his rescue.

'He's cool ... he's cool, Ice, everything's cool. Check this out: right now, me and my boy we kinda loose, man, we was thinking you could make us a deal, you know...'

'A deal?' Ice repeated the word like it sounded dirty.

'Yeah, well, what I mean, man, it's like we kinda down, bro.'

Ice lost patience.

'All right, stop that shit now, right! I know you kinda down. In fact I know you more than that, I know you all fucked up! You and your boy here, you two all fucked up! And you know why? Because you strung up on shit and don't know what the fuck you doing! Look at you!'

Ice sounded vexed at the two young guys.

'Look at them motherfuckers!' He was pointing them out to Early, sitting on the other side.

Both youths were now wishing they hadn't dared approach Ice, but they remained there, quiet and shifting on the spot while Ice berated them.

'That boy!' He pointed to the large-shirted one. 'That fucking boy used to be the fastest, most dangerous pointman I ever seen in my life. When he had the ball in the square, forget it, man. Points like mad!'

The few seconds of recalling his former glory, a reprieve for the unfortunate former wonder man, didn't last long.

'What the fuck happened to you?' Ice was shaking his head. 'Look, get out of my face. I can't even look at you. Just move on, man, try to straighten up. Give up this shit, and get back a life ... y'understand?'

'All right, Ice, man; we hear you. We getting straight; don't worry, Ice... Cool.'

The two young druggies wisely made a silent escape.

Ice watched them hurry away around the corner of the deli. Shaking his head, he told Early:

'It's a waste, I'm telling you. If you ever saw them two kids play ball ... man, I mean like deadly. I even betted on some of them games, betted on points. Made good money too!'

After a few seconds he added:

'Just into college, the fucking kids got in with some fools, started taking shit ... never been the same again, got kicked out from everywhere. A shame, man.'

'Yeah... That shit takes a heavy toll,' Early said.

'That's O.' Ice was looking at a shiny red

Lexus as it came by and parked in front of the van.

Still looking sullen, a herb stick stuck at the corner of his mouth, O quickly checked who was inside the van, then said:

'Dem down by Jelly.'

'How many?' Ice asked.

'Four heads, three or four others, but just make-up boys, friers. Dem will drop out soon as dem see a piece.'

Ice was waiting, looking out through his windscreen at the coming and going in front of the deli. Young boys jostling for girls' appreciation, and no other problems in life.

'Ice, we better catch dem before dem move again. Dem know we after dem.'

'We're moving on them right now. But O, you let me deal with it, all right? Nobody fires unless I say so, you understand?'

O didn't seem very pleased at the injunction; he didn't answer right away.

'Dem will shoot first.'

'You let me go up and run the show, O, man. You cover my back, I go in. All right?'

'All right.' Grudgingly. O looked like he had a personal score to settle.

'Who you got in the car?' Ice asked his man.

'Picka, Metric, James...'

'James!' Ice looked at O like he was crazy. 'I said we was going in to settle things! I don't want no dead bodies, I can't deal with that right now, y'understand?'

Ice really stressed his point.

'I got things on right now, important things, I can't take no heat, not right now... They gonna try to start a shoot-up, but it's not gonna happen. They need it, we don't, OK?'

O nodded eventually.

Ice explained:

'You cover outside, absolute security: nobody goes in, nobody gets out. All right?'

'Yeah, I deal with that.'

'Then let's move. You lead.'

O left right away, released to some kind of action at last.

Early was just keeping to his thoughts while discreetly scanning the surroundings, out of habit. As for Booker, he might as well have been a ghost for the monk-like quietness of the man.

'I got to settle this thing ... until later, you see what I'm saying, Early? I need time.'

'They want your place. If you try to talk sense, they'll see you weak... Then they'll move on you tomorrow.'

'I'll take care of tomorrow ... tomorrow,' Ice told his cousin.

'You sure?'

Ice kicked into gear.

'I been thinking ... about what we talked about... Maybe I got to think about it some more.'

He followed after O's Lexus, already a couple of hundred yards ahead, burning gas.

'But we have a bigger problem to deal with first, you and me ... I got to buy time tonight. Let's go!'

The entrance to Jelly was through a narrow alleyway, next to an all-night bakery; O parked fifty yards farther on, while Ice chose to leave the van on the nearside, behind a delivery truck with a 'Cool Baker' sign painted across it. O came up.

'I want your boys to check out the alley and block the passage once we get inside, all right.' Ice told him.

'Yeah, man.'

'Don't get heavy. Two men outside here, James plus another one, one man at the door. You stay at the door and cover us.'

'Cool.'

O turned to watch a girl emerging from the dimly lit alley.

'See my scout here!'

The girl, in a blond curly wig and striped black denim suit, came up. She glanced at Ice, told O in a dreary voice:

'In the gambling room, at the back. He's got two guys near the bar, a tall one with glasses, plus a dark guy in a white suit.'

O nodded.

'The door?'

'Two guys, one shotgun.'

'See my soldier,' O said to Ice proudly, boosting up the girl.

Ice nodded.

'Good.'

'All right, keep a watch out here; anything move, you call in.'

The girl asked:

'You gonna come down later?'

'Yeah, man, later.'

The girl moved on, stepped inside the bakery.

'We going in,' Ice said, and got out of the van.

Booker stepped out of the sliding door, in a flat leather cap and cord jacket, checked all around, waited for Early to exit before closing the van.

Ice adjusted his wide sports shirt at the back, checking for the bulge. They walked into the alley, one by one, just easy. O had briefed his men, one of them was closing behind. At the door, a knock, two squinting eyes behind the sliding flap. The steel panel opened.

'What's up, home?'

'Cool, Ice, cool.'

The doorman, with plaited hair and short stubble, eyed Early and Booker.

'My cousin,' Ice told him. The man nodded. Early barely acknowledged him.

Another man, in dark glasses, cigarette in

mouth, sat behind a wooden table. The half-unzipped sports bag at his feet was out of sight.

'You see Willy?' Ice asked the doorman while tossing a note on the table.

'Not since yesterday.'

'All right.'

Ice led the way in, opened the soundproof door and stepped into the red light and insistent beat pulsating from the back room. Right away, O dropped out and slipped inside the little crowd hanging alongside the wall.

Ice saw the white-suited man seated at the bar about the same time as the man saw him. He averted his eyes, progressed towards the far wall, easing his way through the dancers. The man slid down from his stool, his eyes searching through the crowd towards the entrance. But the tall man he was looking for had just felt the barrel of O's automatic in his back and was keeping very still. Ice walked right up to the man, smiled coldly and leaned towards him.

'Relax; I come to talk to your boss.'

The man watched his friend arrive, closely followed by a vigilant O. Early and Booker were already waiting in the low-lit area near the door to the gambling room.

'Let's go and play. I feel lucky tonight.'

Ice left the two men in O's care; he quickly patted them while keeping them covered, and walked to the door. He knew the man standing there, bulky with a crown of tight little locks. Some years back he had sponsored a few of his boxing matches.

'What's up, bro?'

'Yeah, cool, Ice... You come to throw away some money? Got too much?'

'No, business is down. I'm gonna have to rob the place,' Ice said, smiling.

The bouncer smiled and nodded, appreciating the joke. Then he noticed the two stern-faced men, O behind them, glanced to his right and there was Early with Booker close by. He looked at Ice again.

'Just a late business meeting, bro... Keep it a restricted access for me, all right?'

The man understood what Ice wanted.

'All right, man; cool.'

The little group, headed by Ice, passed through the door and walked into a different atmosphere. Here the room was narrow, the music not so loud, neon tubes low over a couple of pool tables. Farther down were groups of four or five men sitting, several more standing around them, intensely following the progress of the card games with their heavy stakes. A makeshift bar manned by a wigged brown girl occupied the extreme left corner.

They were bound to draw attention. A well-groomed man at one of the tables on the right froze, his hand hanging in midair with the card he was about to play. Ice was already in front of him.

'What's up, West, got an ace?' Ice didn't sound angry or threatening, yet the man's brow was closed, his eyes still. A heavy-looking set of gold rings and a dark suit gave him the appearance of a rich heir gambling away some of his family wealth.

'Yeah.' The man let the card drop on to the table, slowly.

O and his two captives had stopped a little way behind. West's playing comrades were keeping quiet, avoiding sudden moves. Everyone knew very well why Ice was here.

Then, from behind one of the pool tables, stepped trouble. The man must have stooped low and sneaked around the new-comers. And he had good reason to. On seeing him, O's face became a mask of restrained wrath. With his neat little curls, well-trimmed moustache and, striped silk shirt, he could have been an R'n'B singer. Were it not for the shiny handgun he was pointing...

They always say stick up the biggest nigger first. And the man had instinctively chosen to keep his gun on Booker. But the big man wasn't armed. He just stood there, calm as could be, his dark, still eyes just looking at the gunman, looking at him without anger, like he didn't even see the weapon trained on his massive chest.

'Don't move. You all come here to die?'

It was downright insolence, but Ice turned and looked at him calmly, then asked West:

'You still the boss, West, or you got yourself a spokesman?' Behind West, two men had appeared, standing by the table like sentries on guard duty.

'Easy, Stan!' West said.

Stan had just noticed O's barrel, low, trained on him from the right side, and was now unsure where to point his own. Early and Booker, standing across from O, between Stan and Ice, hadn't moved a muscle since coming into the room.

'Yeah, easy, Stan!' O repeated with a vicious grin.

'Shit happened at my place this morning. Know anything about it, West?' Ice asked, ignoring his man.

But Stan was intense, and intent on causing trouble, it seemed.

'It's not your place no more, we're taking over.'

'You chat hard, bwai,' O remarked, sarcastic.

He would have loved to have shot him right there and then. It had been a hot escape from the burning building.

'You got real gangsters working for you, West.'

Ice was making fun of the man with the gun, a dangerous thing to do in most cases, but he didn't look worried. Early was perfectly still, taking in the scene like he was just another spectator. For a few seconds he locked eyes with one of the men standing behind West, then his gaze slid over to the nervous gunman.

Stan knew Ice was carrying. He could shoot him first, but then O was just waiting for a chance to fill him up with hot lead. The two had been waging a vicious war for the last few weeks, and one of them had to go, that was clear. Then again he could choose to drop O first, but he knew Ice had a reputation for being very fast on the draw. For Stan, it was now down to a matter of speed and choice – the right choice.

O was keeping his weapon firmly on the silk-shirted man. The whole room was watching the deadlock, ready to get low as soon as the first shot was fired. Then Stan heard:

'Put it down, young bwai.'

He turned towards Booker, who was looking at him with no special expression. He took in the size, the blank look, but was too high and too far involved to be wise. He moved his gun Booker's way. Just like Booker knew he would.

'Who the fuck you talking to?' Stan sounded real dangerous.

'You curse like a big man,' Booker remarked, his voice smoothly insulting.

That got Stan mad. He levelled his gun on the big bearded man, too foolish to realise he was being baited.

'You wan' dead!'

'Hey, Stan, you have a match?' O asked, very stinging in tone.

Stan turned to curse him. Mistake...

No one, not even Early, had seen Booker pick it up, but suddenly a pool ball had sprung from his hand and was smashing at full speed into Stan's face, hard.

Shocked, the gunman reeled backward, blood spluttering from his cut mouth. O seemed to have been watching for his chance; in an instant he was over him like a cat on a trapped mouse, grabbed the gun from the wounded man and hit him with his own butt on the forehead, just for good measure. Another gash appeared, more blood spilled over Stan's face, then he dropped on the floor like a bag of cement.

'You fuck up now, boy!' O sneered over the fallen body, after picking up the man's gun.

'You should really be more careful who you employ, West.' Ice shook his head.

West looked at Ice, holding the stare. For a few seconds he dropped his blank mask and shot Ice a glance of undisguised fury. He knew he had been outplayed and now his life was in Ice's hands. The two men standing guard behind him were keeping very still.

'So, you wanna tell me about that fire-bomb this morning?'

Ice's voice had that very edgy tone now.

West's eyes travelled from Ice to Early, to Booker, then back to Ice. Then he said slowly:

'It's got nothing to do with me.'

'Your clown here burned down my place!'

'I didn't send him,' West said simply.

Ice glared at him.

'West, don't fuck with me. You want my business, you come out like a man.'

West knew he was in a bad spot. He sighed and shook his head.

'I heard Stan been hitting your business but it's not down to me; I didn't send him.'

Ice let a few seconds pass. He shook his head, sounding almost amused:

'See, that's what I'm talking about: you got no control over guys like that working for you.' He paused, then added: 'That's very dangerous, West, it could cause you some serious prejudice.'

Everyone in the room understood exactly what Ice was saying. West was known as a bigmouth, but right now he seemed as meek as a lamb.

'Stan's too hot headed, he don't listen.'

Ice said nothing for a moment. He looked around him. Everybody knew West had been talking bad, about how he was going to take over the block from Ice. They also knew that Ice had been holding back. Now they all expected West to end up in a pool of blood somewhere on a wasteland. But Ice looked like he was buying West's lie, and that was surprising.

'All right, then we take out Stan and the problem will go away, right?'

West shrugged.

'Like I said, it's not down to me, man.'

'Cool,' Ice said. 'Since you say so; we'll leave the innocents alone and just take the guilty.'

Ice motioned to Stan lying on the floor, blood seeping from his mouth.

'Bring him along!'

Booker simply grabbed the man by the shirt around the back of the neck and dragged him through the door and out. O was covering the room from the door, waiting for Early and Ice to move out.

'Well, we got it sorted out then, West ... I'll see you around,' Ice told the man with the cards before leaving the room.

Outside, O's men had done their job well – the whole place was discreetly isolated from the street. Ice led the way back to the van, slid the door open. Booker had Stan's limp body slung over his shoulder, looking easy, like a man just back from a hunt. He dropped him inside, climbed up.

As Booker was about to close the sliding

door, someone appeared out of the alley and he stopped. His keen eyes quickly clocked the man in a suit walking up in rapid strides. Booker stepped out. Early and Ice had seen him too. The man had his hands out, so Booker relaxed and waited. They came eye to eye in the street lighting: the grey-suited young man who'd been standing behind West, inside the den.

He stopped a few yards away, realising that Booker would never let him get to where he was going.

'Early!' he called out.

Behind Booker, after a few seconds, Early said quietly:

'Let him through.'

Booker moved smoothly to the right, watching the man as he moved towards the van window. He must have been in his early twenties, although the low stubble covering his cheeks and the composure in his moves spoke of a few years more.

'Respeck, Don,' the man told Early.

Though he hadn't been sure a few minutes earlier, back inside, something tugged at his memory, and Early looked deeper into the youth's eyes. He got it right.

'Danny?'

The half-smile confirmed it. Early nodded, amused at the fortuitous meeting.

'Yeah... Long time.'

'Fe real.' Early nodded. 'What you doing

here, Danny, man? When you leave Jamaica?'

Danny shrugged.

'Two years now, but I did stay in Texas for a while.'

'Texas?' Early repeated.

Ice had been listening from his seat. He asked Early:

'You know him?'

Early nodded.

'His sister have Wally first pickney. Danny's family.'

That was good enough for Ice. He asked the youth:

'You work for West, home?'

Danny looked at him.

'I did couple things with him; but right now, certain tings ah go down.'

Ice motioned inside the van behind him.

'Your friend in there did it alone or West send him?'

Danny made a face, answered Ice:

'That boy is not my friend: him head all fucked up.'

He looked at Early

'We ha fe talk, Don. You can meet me at Nine O Spade on Uttica in one hour?'

'Cool, one hour.'

'All right.' Danny turned on his heels, but didn't go back inside.

Nine O Spade was a late hanging-out place

and, since it was only nine something, too early for the usual customers, it was nice and quiet. None of the heavy crews were there; they would drift in around one. Only a few couples sipping and sharing secrets, plus a few hungry types filling their rumbling stomachs. Behind the counter at the back, a large lady with a blue-and-white scarf on her head was watching a loud episode of her favourite soap.

Early had his back to the street. Booker always liked to sit facing the entrance wherever he went. A round of thick iced Irish Moss for the little group. Ice asked Danny:

'So, who's behind him?'

'Nobody, nobody local.' Danny took a sip. 'That boy was dealing shit in Maryland but the cops run him out. I buck him up one time in a place down in the West Bronx, help him out of it.' Danny smiled.

'So he really thinks he's gonna take over my business?' Ice sounded more incredulous than angry at the insolence.

'West have a contact with some Cuban gangsta. The guy can get high-quality stuff, nuff of it ... but him don't have a place to sell it. Him shoot a man who try to rob him in the Bronx, so him can't go back there. The man dem looking for him. Him looking for a base.'

'Yeah?' Ice smirked. 'I'm gonna help him find a base, a permanent one too... In a deep hole somewhere in the countryside!'

Early asked:

'What's the play, Danny?'

The youth shook his head.

'The guy rotten, Don; him give up anybody if that can help him. Him don't have no heart, man!'

'Him work for the police?' Early enquired.

'Him have certain tings ah gwan with them, I know that.'

'What about that boy, Stan?' Ice asked.

Danny kissed his teeth.

'The boy ah fool, man; him head full a drugs, him well mash up already. Him do anything West tell him to do. West give him the drugs and use him.'

Ice shook his head.

'I feel I got to take care of my friend West.' He nodded. 'Pretty soon...'

Then Danny said:

'Don't worry about West, I have him line up already long time.'

Early looked at the youth.

'You got problems with him?'

'No,' Danny answered. 'But him causing a lot of static everywhere. Him just taking space for nothing.'

Early remembered Danny just out of secondary school, with a dimple in his chin and a love of books and cricket. Nowadays Danny was somewhat harder.

'It would be better I run the operations,

better for me ... and better for you, Don.'

Early looked at Ice, then at Danny. The younger man told him:

'I never know West was going against your business, Don. I never even know brother Ice. I just come up from down south last month. The bwai gimme a job to do security at one hotel him running; but I have better things planned. Right now, I feel I can take over that bwai runnings and link up with the man dem. Wha you ah say?'

Early and Ice listened. It sounded interesting.

'What about the rest of them?'

Danny explained:

'Him have about a dozen youths running with him but only about five are real soldiers. I talk to them, they will follow me, no problem.

Ice was finding the idea a simple and effective one. Just one thing:

'You know where he hides the stuff?'

This time Danny broke into a wide grin.

'Yeah ... but I got better than that: I got my own link to his Cuban contact!'

Ice was impressed. He felt happy at the good fortune of meeting Danny. Now, not only he could solve an immediate problem but he also had an unexpected break for the future.

'You know something, Danny: I think you right. It'd be better if you run things.'

Now they were both looking at Early, watching the amused glint in his eyes.

'I never thought I find you in New York working with Ice's enemy,' he said to the youth. 'But it could turn out very good for everybody.'

Ice grinned wickedly and added:

'Yeah, except for West!'

'Eh-eh...' Danny laughed.

'Now, about this job I was talking about; this is what I need done...' Ice's face had already lost the fun vibe.

Back in the van, O had been looking after Stan. West's man had been having a conversation with his enemy, apparently. Ice found him tied up hands and feet, O leaning over him with his lit lighter in his hand. The smell of burning told it all.

'I told you to watch him,' Ice told his lieutenant from the driver's seat.

'I'm watching him. Him play with fire, so him must get burn,' O stated without humour.

Ice picked up his phone and dialled. He got through after a couple of trials.

'Yeah ... what you got?... Yo, you let me worry about that! Just give me what I need, all right ... I'm in a rush.'

Ice wasn't inclined to patience tonight, couldn't afford it. He listened, nodding to himself.

'Yeah, I got it ... yeah, yeah, I know that... What he look like?... Hmm... OK, don't worry about it, you call me tomorrow, all right? Yeah, you be safe out there.'

Switching off, Ice turned to Early.

'We're on, got a target.'

Then he dialled again, waited for the connection.

'Boogy? What? Yo, girl, get off the line and get me Boogy right now!'

Ice kissed his teeth, shook his head in frustration.

'That's one thing I hate,' he said. 'Nigger got a phone but leaves it with his girl!'

Someone spoke into the phone.

'Boogy, man, you supposed to be on stand-by, what the fuck you doing?... What? No, no, I don't want to hear that shit. You go to take a shit, you have the phone with you, all right?... Just don't do that again, it gets me real nervous...'

There must have been excuses from the other end. Ice cooled down.

'Right, I got a mission for you. You go to the address I'm gonna give you. You check it out, but you don't show yourself. Find out who lives there but keep away, just watch the place. I'm looking for a guy ... about six-three, two hundred pounds, long hair with a ponytail. He's hiding down there. You check out the place, then you call me and let me know. Take a man with you, but no fuck-up.

You just watch and report, get it? Right, you go right now, report as soon as you know the set-up... Take this address...'

Ice gave a location then cut off. He told Early:

'Fucking guy's hiding from the mob, looks like. He was supposed to be infiltrating Sal's organisation but was apparently working for himself too. The story is like this: the cop had set Sal up on a big shipment from some Chinese kids. Sal's boys robbed it. But then the cop, he decided to set him up, let his friend bust him then take back the coke. Smart guy, eh?'

Things like that happened every day, in Miami as well as New York. Early asked:

'You sure about your source?'

Ice smiled.

'He's a greedy fucker but very reliable. And the story starts to make sense.'

That was true. Early was getting to understand that Lisa had stepped into something she didn't know anything about. But who was the girl who had brought her there? That was the key to it all, he felt.

'We need answers from that cop.'

'He'll talk, don't worry. Right now, we just wait till we sure the guy's in, then we move on him.'

From the back, O called out.

'Ice, make we finish off this bwai and dump him.'

With O as judge and jury, the unfortunate Stan was already sentenced.

Ice turned around but didn't answer. He asked Early:

'What you think?'

As usual, Early waited a little before answering.

'It don't matter to me. His boss is your problem.'

Ice nodded.

'Yeah, but your boy Danny's gonna fix that, right?'

'Danny's got a hand to play. He'll take care of it.'

'Right.' Ice called out to O: 'Bring your friend over here.'

Roughly, O grabbed Stan by the collar and pulled him up on his knees, yanked him to the space behind the front seat. Even in the dim light, it was clear that Stan was in a bad way. A couple of his front teeth had been knocked out by Booker's pool ball; a bloody gash from O's gun butt swelled his forehead. His silk shirt was torn and open on his thin chest, where a flame had left dark and swollen burn marks.

'You're in a bad way, boy,' Ice remarked.

Like all drug addicts, in pain and fear his bravado had been replaced by a pitiful look, and his eyes were wide open in terror.

'It was West... It was him ... I swear,' Stan mumbled.

'West told you to burn down my place?' Ice asked, no anger showing in his voice.

'Yeah... Yeah.'

'He said he never told you that. Said you did it on your own,' Ice stated, stern as a district attorney.

Stan got all agitated, shifted on the spot, as much as his tied-up limbs allowed him to.

'No, man, he lied! He sent me! I swear, he told me to do it!'

From behind, O slapped him on the back of the head.

'But you shot after my brethren last week outside the pool hall! You fucking dog!'

O sounded really pissed off at the man. The business he was running for Ice had been under attack for weeks, and it was Stan's hand striking the blows, that was all he knew. He told Ice:

'Make we kill him and done. Let me deal with him.' A sincerely eager plea.

Ice looked at Stan, knowing the prisoner had his guts knotted with fear now.

'Looks like my boy here wants your blood. What can I do?'

'I was just following orders, but it's West, Don, he's after your business. I'm begging you, Don, gimme a break. I do anything you want.'

'You all fucked up, Stan, your brain's full of shit. You don't even know what you doing. West tells you to hit me and you do it? You don't know who I am?'

'I know, Don, but West would have kill me if I refused... He was the boss; you can understand that, Don!'

'And now he sold you out, and you gonna die because of him.'

'Please, don't kill me, man. Gimme a chance!'

That got him a hard thump on the head from O.

'A chance? You give we a chance to come out of the fucking fire this morning? You was out to burn me up, you bloodclaat!'

Stan cried out in pain; he was crying loudly now.

'I'm sorry, man. Sorry. I ... I'll do anything you want, tell me what you want me to do, anything ... I'll do it for you, Don...'

'Yeah?' Ice asked him.

There was hope there, and Stan grabbed at the straw like a drowning man.

'Anything, I swear. Just gimme a chance, I can do anything.'

'You a fucking crackhead! You fe dead,' O said coldly.

Ice was his only ray of hope of leaving the van alive, that much was clear to Stan. He tried to stop crying.

'Try me, I'll do what you say, Don...' An idea surfaced in his terror-stricken mind. 'I'll kill him, I'll kill him for you. Yeah, I can do it!'

Ice smiled, not very warmly, but it was sunshine to Stan.

'West gave you up to me; he wouldn't let you get near him again. In fact, if I don't kill you, he will, you know that.'

Stan thought about it for a second and realised it was true.

'But ... but I can help you to get him ... I know everything about him; where he sleeps, who he do business with, I know his women... I can help you take him down.'

Ice thought about it. He was a hard man, used to seeing and dealing death. But he liked to think he only took life when there was no other way. He could have Stan killed right away and not worry about it ever again, but then the man might be of some use soon. He sighed.

'I don't want to give you a break and regret it later, boy...'

'You won't regret it, Don... You'll never regret it, just let me help you. I'll do what you want me to do...'

A tiny flame was now burning inside Stan's cold guts.

'All right, this is what you gonna do; you give my boy here a number. Give him a number where I can reach you day and night. Y'understand?'

'Yeah, yeah ... I got a number.' Stan was breathing hard, swallowing like a sheep in the dry season.

'Anyhow, I call you once and you don't answer, or anybody else answer ... you won't see the next day, got that?'

'Yes, Don, don't worry, I'll wait for your call, day and night.' Stan sounded like he was gonna hug that phone like a baby.

'And don't forget: you owe me a life, and you will pay your debt.' In Ice's stare was a promise, a guarantee, and Stan had no doubt about it.

'I owe you a life,' Stan repeated meekly.

Ice nodded.

'Good.' He looked for O's cold and disapproving gaze. 'Take his number and let him go.'

O did as he was told; that was the way things were – Ice had plans for the boy. Yet somehow, O reflected, he might still just get a chance to deal with Stan, later on.

'You better leave the area, you hear? Don't show yourself, don't go anywhere. Lock yourself up someplace until I call.'

'Yes, Don, I'll do it. Nobody's gonna see me. I'll be there when you call, any time.'

Stan was rubbing his wrists, licking his dry lips, overwhelmed by gratitude.

'Go and fix yourself up,' Ice told the reprieved man.

'Yes, I'll take care of that, Don.' Stan nodded. 'And ... thanks, Don, thanks.'

'Later,' Ice replied without even looking back. His mind was already on other things.

Stan saw Booker open the sliding door and was out in a flash. Without a look or a goodbye to O.

'I'm hungry. Let's pick up some food and go home until my boy reports,' Ice said.

The car was parked about a block away from the house. Ice saw the man leaning against it before he got there.

'What the fuck?'

Early had seen him too, a dark silhouette in a suit, not hiding, just waiting.

'Friend?' he asked.

O had come up to check the matter out. He said:

'It's that fucking cop!'

Booker looked through the windscreen too but didn't say anything. Ice parked his van just behind the car.

'You tink him come alone?' O asked, scanning the surroundings for any hidden police presence. His hand was already slipping around the gun in his waist. But the road was quiet.

'He comes to talk. Just chill. I'll see what he wants.'

Ice exited the van and walked to the car. The two men stood a yard apart.

'You come home late, Ice,' Burrows said.

'Yeah, well, I'm on a night shift,' Ice answered, wondering what the policeman wanted with him at this late hour.

'Working hard, eh?'

Ice shrugged. 'By the sweat of my brow...' Then he said: 'You could have called me, saved you hanging around. This is a rough neighbourhood.'

'Yeah, it was already rough when I was growing up back then, a couple blocks from here.'

'So, you got homesick?'

Burrows straightened up, shook his head.

'No... We got to talk. You wanna get in the car?'

Ice made a face.

'I usually avoid getting inside cops' cars. I hope it's a private invitation.'

'I'm off duty. Come on.'

Burrows opened his door and got in. Ice went around, joined him inside the vehicle.

'What you doing?' Burrows asked, after watching Ice looking under the dash, running his hands around the edges of the seat.

'My voice don't sound good on tape...'

Burrows smiled, shook his head.

'I'm a cop but not that kind, Ice; you know that. This is just a man-to-man conversation, OK?'

'OK,' Ice said.

Burrows and he had known each other for years. The man was a straight cop. Growing up in the projects, he'd joined the police but somehow had kept his reputation as a man of his word. Every local hustler knew that much.

'I guess it's got to be important for you to be out on the street this time of night when you're not working. Your wife might think you got a girl out there...'

'I been divorced for a while now, Ice. And yes, it is important ... to you.'

Ice was curious now.

'So, what's up?'

Burrows knew he now had the younger man's attention. He started:

'OK, I'm gonna tell you what I know, then you can tell me if you know about it or not...'

'All right.'

There was a pause, as if Burrows was choosing his words, the best way to put it.

'We've been picking up bodies on the doorstep of our friend Sal Scaffone. His men are being killed and delivered to him. Apparently, he's having a little dispute with another mob guy from Queens. You heard about that?'

'If it happens in Brooklyn, I hear about it,' Ice said simply.

The cop went on.

'Right. We thought it was another one of these blood feuds between wiseguys, like it happens every ten years or so. Then I found out that Sal has been under surveillance by the DEA for a while. They think he's branched out into drugs too...'

Ice could feel Burrows looking straight in his eyes, like he could read something there.

He said:

'Why you telling me all that? I'm a black man, I don't do business with mob guys, you know that. Don't trust them, don't like them. They could wipe each other out, I wouldn't care.'

Burrows nodded.

'Yeah, I know... But I'll tell you another story, maybe you'll understand why I wanted to talk to you.'

Ice waited. Burrows checked his rear-view mirror, glanced around before going on.

'A week ago, they picked up this girl on the Latino side of east New York. She'd been shot and dumped. They left her for dead but she survived, the doctors saved her. She had no papers, nothing on her, nobody knew who she was. Somebody took the trouble of burning her fingertips with acid... It looked like somebody wanted her dead real bad. Shot her seven times. But she made it, though, a real miracle.'

Ice didn't react, waited for the cop to go on.

'So, the girl makes it to the hospital, then things start to happen... A couple of nights later, a gunman gets to her room in intensive care and tries to finish her off. But he didn't find her there. You know why? Because she had left.'

Burrows sighed.

'I mean, disappeared! Girl was just about alive, couldn't walk ... the doctor said she's paralysed from the neck down, she got a bullet close to the spine... How the hell the girl left the hospital nobody knows, but she simply vanished. And nobody seen her since.'

Ice could feel the policeman's gaze.

'Weird story,' he said, because it looked like he was expected to say something.

'Yeah, that's what I said too.' Burrows shook his head. 'I got interested but couldn't get no leads Then the next day, these two FBI agents come over to my office. Apparently the FBI was on the case too, but you must know agencies usually don't cooperate, so the DEA were doing their thing, the FBI doing their own too. Anyway, these guys come over, with a photofit, and tell me the girl in the hospital had been seen at Sal's place the day before she was found shot. Imagine that.'

Ice was getting more and more interested, but his face remained blank.

'Got a break there,' he said simply.

'Right, talk about a break. I didn't know who the girl was but now the Bureau guys wanted to find her 'cause they were sure Sal had something to do with her shooting and they wanted her to testify. Since the girl looked local, kinda Latina or something like that, they asked me to try everything to find her. So I'm with this case going nowhere, then my partner digged up a picture from the files, looking just like the photofit the Bureau guys left me. It was the same girl.'

'Yeah?' Ice was following the police investigation step by step; he had no choice.

'Oh, yeah, same girl. Pretty girl too; about twenty-two years of age, long, dark curly hair, beautiful girl.'

'So you fell in love?' Ice sneered.

'I could have,' Burrows admitted. 'But I'm too old for that shit, Ice... Anyway, we didn't have nothing in the file apart from that photograph, nothing at all. It was just filed because some cop saw her around a known crime figure and took her picture, just in case. But there was a name.'

'Hm?' Ice couldn't say more than that.

'Oh, yeah...' Burrows held the suspense a few seconds longer. 'Lisa.'

'Lisa?'

'Lisa Hanley,' the policeman said quietly, like he didn't want the name overheard outside the confines of the car.

A silence floated around the two men. Until Ice asked:

'So you came to see me just because the girl's name is Hanley?'

'I came to see you because I remembered a very beautiful woman who used to live off Crown Heights – Jennifer Hanley. One of the prettiest girls in the whole school, that's what everybody used to say about your mother...'

Ice didn't have to answer anything to that. And he didn't especially like to hear about his mother, but it was a compliment. Burrows had told him before, when they had first got acquainted, that he had been one of his mother's fervent admirers.

'So ... what d'you want from me?' he asked.

Burrows looked away for a moment.

'Look, Ice, I don't know exactly what the story is about, but I think you're involved somehow. I came to talk to you because this is heavy, maybe a little too heavy for you. And I don't want to find you at the centre of a murder scene one of these days, you understand what I'm saying?'

Ice understood, but he knew Burrows was thinking as a cop, a friendly cop but a cop.

'Yeah. And I appreciate you taking the time to come and tell me this story.'

Both men, the older cop and the young hustler, read each other for a few seconds. Then Burrows smiled.

'I knew you'd react like that, Ice, but I had to come over to ask you to let it go.'

'Let it go?'

'Yeah ... let it go, man. 'Cause you got lucky so far, but them mob guys ain't no fools, not for long anyway. And I don't want an open war between you and them on the streets of Brooklyn.'

Ice smiled.

'Wouldn't look good for you, right?'

Burrows shook his head, serious.

'I got about six or seven years to go before I hand in my badge. I ain't worried about my career. But you got to worry about your life. It ain't the same thing.'

'I heard you, man. Like I said, I appreciate you letting me know all this.'

'One more thing; if the FBI can get the girl, they think they can get Sal to testify against his uncle, the big boss, to get himself off the hook. That way they can close down the mob operations in Brooklyn. The DEA wants her too, 'cause they lost an agent inside Sal's place. The last person they heard talking to him was Lisa.'

Burrows waited for Ice to think about all this. He said:

'She's at the centre of the play, Ice. And this is a major one.'

Burrows kept his gaze steady on Ice's face for a moment before going on.

'Sal's totally off limits, that's what I came to tell you. Let it go.'

Ice nodded.

'Sure sounds heavy,' he said. 'Now, thanks for coming but I really got to go. I got food waiting.'

'OK, Ice. I guess I'll see you around.'

Burrows nodded.

'Yeah, you will.' Ice started opening the door to get out.

'One last thing, home.'

Ice waited.

'You tell Early to take his sister home. New York's climate's not healthy for him.'

The hard stare between them was short but intense. Now each one of them knew as much as the other.

'Be safe out there now,' Ice said simply, picking up on the cops' usual farewell to those leaving for street patrol.

'You too, Ice.' Burrows started his engine.

By the time Ice got inside the van, the dark car had already turned around and was speeding away.

'What's it about?' Early asked, noticing his cousin's serious face.

'The weather,' Ice said enigmatically, kicking his engine alive.

G-man always drove like that. He was the most easygoing, laid-back kind of man most of the time, but turned into a happy maniac as soon as he sat behind the wheel of a car. Then his round, dark features tightened and his eyes became scanners, alert, viewing every other vehicle as a potential opponent.

'Watcha now, man; ease up 'pon the speed, seen?' Danny said for the second time in fifteen minutes.

'I not driving fast!' G-man glanced at his friend.

Danny squinted.

'You not driving fast? You drive like a bank robber. And you a swerve in and out like you fucking drunk!'

'No, man; dis is proactive driving, yuh nuh know?'

'Proactive?' Danny looked at the driver like he was crazy.

'Yeah, man; it means you anticipate what the other car gwan do before them do it. You always keep one move ahead.'

'What?' Danny shook his head. 'Where you get that from?'

'Me have a cousin who ah police driver back ah Yard ... him teach me that.'

Danny knew his best friend was something of a character, always inventing the wildest antics and developing theories to support them.

He sighed.

'Look, forget proactive and all that shit. We deh'pon a mission and I don't want we get pull up because you drive like a madman, you understand? Slow down, man!'

Reluctantly, G-man eased up on the gas pedal.

It was going on 2.30 in the morning. The shine from a light shower earlier on had the tarmac glistening like a ribbon under the lights of the causeway. Danny and G-man had spent a couple of hours at a local club, rolling spliffs and sipping on Guinness before driving down to visit a couple of girls they had met earlier in the day. As it happened, when they got there they found three guys already sitting in the living room with the girls, drinking liquor and acting like they owned the apartment. Danny had simply glanced at the tall brown girl with the short perm and broad hips who'd asked him to pass by.

'Listen, now; I don't like mix-up, you understand?'

G-man was already sitting down, relaxed as ever, getting into the cop movie on the wide-screen TV. He seemed unconcerned by the presence of the other guys.

'They just friends from down the block, they cool,' the girl said.

Danny was finding the three loudly dressed, glassy-eyed local young bucks less than cool. They were also throwing glances towards the two newcomers, especially Danny, realising these were Jamaican characters, notoriously bad-tempered and jealous types. Danny got closer to the girl.

'I really thought you wanted me and you to get together, you know?' he told the girl in a low voice, his eyes stressing the word 'together'.

'Yeah, that's what I wanted too.' The girl smiled, responding to Danny's smooth angle.

'So, what; you changed your mind? 'Cause I really like you and I been waiting all day to spend time with you,' the charmer pushed on.

This time, the girl cocked her head sideways a little, bit her bottom lip and asked:

'You been thinking about that all day?'

Danny's eyes were two shiny snakes, sliding over the girl's high breasts under the cotton vest, around the generous curves of her jeans.

'Mm-hm; I been thinking about that all day ... and now I see you, I'm getting real thirsty. You know what I'm saying?'

The girl's smile got suggestive. She ran her forefinger, slowly, over Danny's cheek, then smoothly turned from the doorstep where she stood.

'You all have to excuse us now, we got business to deal with. I see you later, all right?'

The three guys looked up at the girl. One quick glance at Danny's unkind face next to her and they picked up their drinks and got up to leave, muttering, 'Cool, man, no problem ... check you out later.'

The other girl, shorter but just as fit looking in a short white skirt and tight red top, was holding on to a half-spliff left by the guests. Danny couldn't for the life of him remember either of the two girls' names, but it didn't matter now.

'Throw way that, baby girl, ah we have the lick!' he called out. 'G, give her a spliff; sexy girl like that shouldn't smoke nothing but high grade! No true?'

The girl grinned at the compliment.

'Fe real, star,' G-man said, pulled out a plastic bag from his trouser pocket and proceeded to roll up a cone, one eye on the movie, the other on the girl in red and her voluminous thighs.

About one hour later, G-man was still in the living room while Danny had progressed to the spacious upstairs bedroom, but both were getting busy doing acrobatics, drawing hearty moans and breathless little squeaks from their hosts. Two hours later, it was time to roll.

'You know whe the place deh?' G-man asked.

'Yeah, man, we soon get there.'

Neither of the two was familiar with the borough they were driving through, but then again a month spent in Brooklyn had not been much to get used to their new patch. After leaving Tivoli Gardens for Dallas a year before, the pair were ready to explore and conquer absolutely any territory.

G-man was quiet for a moment, then asked:

'You know why Early want to hit dem man deh?'

'Not really, you know. Early is a man who don't talk a lot ... but if him say do it, then I do it.'

G-man waited a little.

'So, we gwan work for Early?'

Danny turned sideways to look at the driver, his devoted childhood friend and trusted sidekick. He said:

'We gwan work fe weself.'

He could see G-man didn't quite get the whole picture.

'Check this out: from we get to New York we don't get a break. We just make couple dollars covering that fool West, but dis not getting we nowhere. But you know what: West draw a bad card and is we gwan benefit from it, you nuh see it?'

It sounded attractive to G-man. Danny asked him:

'Tell me something; you ever get five grands since you come over? Tonight we get paid in advance, my youth. Ah so Early stay. Me and him ah family, man.'

For G-man, cash was the best testimony to good leadership. He said:

'Early wicked, man.'

Danny agreed.

'You see from me meet Early tonight, ev'ryting safe now. Me and you cool, G-man, we gwan make nuff dollars, trust me! Take a left.'

Five minutes later, G-man parked his

Pontiac in the shadow of a metal over-ground train bridge.

'You sure it's the right place?' he asked.

'Yeah, man.'

Danny was looking at something on the other side of the street, a little way down the road. The area was quiet, not many pedestrians, few cars driving on either side of the avenue.

'So how you wanna do this?' G-man asked again.

He was vaguely aware of the mission, knowing only that Danny always had a clear idea of what he was going to do before he did it.

Not a rash man, though a determined one, Danny knew there was only one right way to deal with the particular job he'd been given tonight. He told G-man:

'You see the road we come from, to the right over there, that's the way we going out again. I want you just go up first, turn round to the other side under the train line then come back up this way. Drive slowly, you hear?'

'Yeah, man.'

'All right.'

Danny opened the door, went round to the boot. He came back inside but sat at the back of the car with a long canvas bag. G-man watched him unzip it, pull out a long plastic tube, unfold it.

'Ah whe the raas you get this, man?'

Danny flashed a little grin under the dim streaked light filtering under the bridge.

'A man who couldn't pay me for some shit get me this. I know I was gonna need it some day!'

'You know how to use it?'

This time Danny looked at his friend, explained:

'You see like you have a police driver cousin, I have soldier uncle, a sergeant.'

G-man was looking at the weapon, impressed. A keen and knowledgeable movie fanatic, he right away found a reference.

'Hey, you' member that movie whe the man shoot down a helico with one ah dem? Whe the flim call again?'

Danny didn't know the film G-man was talking about, neither did he particularly care right now; he had a job to do for Early and he intended to do it perfectly well.

'It's Early tell you to blow up that place with that ting?' G-man asked.

Danny was adjusting the sight, checking the launcher, getting comfortable with it.

'Him seh fe hit the place; so we gwan hit the place.'

'But, Danny: you ever use that ting before?'

G-man seemed a little worried by the war tool his friend was holding. Danny looked at his partner.

'Don't worry about that, man, just

concentrate on driving.'

The mean-looking tube took up most of the length of the back seat. Danny said:

'Bring down that back window.'

G-man complied, pressed the electric switch operating the window behind Danny.

'All right, mek we do it, man: drive!'

Danny kept the weapon low, watching everything around them, calculating the right time to fire, knowing that he would have, literally, only one shot at it. A smooth approach, a straight hit and a swift exit: that was the only way. G-man took the Pontiac nicely around the bend under the rail arch, drove back up, slowly, as required by Danny.

Ten yards before the target, Danny raised the tube level with the car window, ready to aim. He had positioned himself steadily, back against the door behind him, feet solidly wedged against the back of the front seat and the other door. One last look around to check for activity and he levelled the tube. The neatly decorated building with the pretty little potted trees in front came into view.

'Steady,' Danny said.

Then he pressed the trigger. The whoosh sound took him a little by surprise, but there was no time to think about it. A flame rushed out of the back as the rocket left the tube and hit the front of the café with full force. G-man and Danny didn't see much of the damage but the noise alone was enough to tell them the hit had been performed; an explosion like the neighbourhood had never experienced.

A sharp turn ten yards down behind a delivery truck into a side road, and they moved on.

'Keep driving normally, man, all the way back to Brooklyn,' Danny instructed his driver.

Monday

Booker was on to his third pancake, and visibly enjoying it. A childhood spent scavenging the hard, hot turf of western Kingston ghettoes had turned him into a man with a hunger never quite satisfied. He ate more than his fill nowadays, and earned enough never to want for anything, but Booker couldn't help it. He always ate as if it all could end suddenly and he could find himself back out there on the deadly streets starving again.

Early and Ice had finished breakfast and were watching Dr Willard checking out Lisa from the kitchen. The tall, silver-haired white man had been coming to the house every two days. This morning, he was gently feeling her limbs, massaging the joints, watching for any reaction. Lisa's gaze was fixed straight on the man, but it was impossible to tell whether she appreciated what he was trying to do for her or not. Marylee sat next to them, watching, trying to catch any sign of response from the paralysed girl.

Dr Willard got up and went behind the chair, started applying his fingers to the back of Lisa's head and neck, feeling around the spine, pressing lightly on her shoulder muscles.

'We have to move her,' Ice said.

Early didn't answer but knew his cousin was right.

'That cop's cool with me but he's a cop all the same. The FBI and the DEA are looking for her; we can't take a chance thinking he won't talk.'

'Yeah, you're right,' Early agreed.

He was looking at his little sister, so beautiful, so lively just a short two weeks earlier when she flew out of Miami. It was so hard to look at her now, disfigured, silent and still. Worse to think she might remain like that for the rest of her life. A pool of cold anger had been ebbing at the pit of Early's stomach ever since he had arrived in town and seen the damage wrought on his sister.

'Marylee got an aunt living out in Trenton.

We gonna drive down there and leave both of them there until this business is sorted out.'

Early nodded.

'Yeah, best to get your wife out of the way too; just in case...'

Ice's phone rang; he opened it and listened.

'All right, get another team out there, send the others back home. He's bound to show up soon. Call me when it's on.'

Early waited for the news.

'The cop's been out all night, but he'll be back soon. He's been moving only at night. My boys got the area tied up,' Ice explained.

'Hm... We got to talk to that guy; he's at the centre of all this. Then we'll deal with the mob guy.'

Ice sneered.

'Things gonna move on that side too; your boy did a good job last night.'

'Yeah ... I told you Danny's a good soldier. We got them all confused, now the other side's gonna have to retaliate. All we got to do is keep watch on the place and wait till the boy sticks his head out.'

'I got a team on surveillance down there. I think Sal's gonna try to shake off his police dogs soon. That's when we make our move on him.'

'Give her the power, Lord, give your child the power.'

From the living room, the voice was strong but gentle. It drew Ice to turn and come over to the door. Dr Willard was squatting in front of Lisa, holding her face in his hands. His eyes, intense, deep, were looking into Lisa's own.

'Be merciful, O God, be merciful unto your suffering child.'

Ice watched. It was bringing back memories of younger days, when his mother used to drag him to the Brooklyn Baptist Chapel on Sunday mornings. Back then, Ice didn't really enjoy it but he had to go all the same. His mama was a strong-willed lady and seemed to greatly enjoy the loud preaching there. It all seemed very noisy and a little intimidating to the ten-year-old boy. Dr Willard was calling on the Lord right now, just like the Baptist preachers invoked Him all those years ago.

'Heal your child, Father, let her overcome the hurt, the pain, and give her strength to raise her spirit.'

When Marylee had first brought the surgeon the previous week, Early and Ice didn't trust him much but needed his expertise on Lisa's condition. Though he explained honestly that he was not a nerve specialist, Dr Willard surprised the two men by stating that, in his humble opinion, her paralysis was not due to any damage to her brain or spine but rather resulted from a nervous block. He thought that the brutality of the shooting had caused her nervous system to go into seizure, as if her brain had switched off and frozen the nerve centres controlling her vital functions.

To Early's enquiry as to whether his sister would walk again, the white doctor said that he thought she would, but only when the psychological trauma she had suffered was resolved. Only Lisa could do that, he said. This puzzled Early and Ice. Marylee agreed with Dr Willard when he said prayer would be a great help, that Lisa's spirit was hurt much more than her body.

Behind him, Ice heard Booker say to Early:

'That white man sound like him have a strong spirit in him.'

As Dr Willard let go of Lisa's face, he said firmly:

'God loves you, Lisa ... you know God loves you!' The man gently took the young woman's hands in his.

Then Marylee gasped:

'Oh my God, she's crying! She's crying!'

Alerted, Early came to join Ice, looking at the scene. Lisa's frail chest was heaving, breath pumping strongly through her slender body.

Then Early looked down and saw it: Dr Willard's hands were holding Lisa's own and her fingers were slowly but visibly squeezing his. Just enough to hold on to his, but they were moving. The two men watched in shock.

'Almighty Lord, give her the power, restore her spirit, we pray, O Lord, for only You can do it. Heal her, let her be free, let Lisa be free again, O Lord!'

Dr Willard had little beads of sweat over his forehead. He was smiling.

'That's good, Lisa,' he said. 'You can do it, you can move again, right?'

'That's right!' Marylee's eyes were dropping tiny tears, her face beaming. 'You can move again, my girl ... you gonna be all right, baby!'

Lisa was breathing deeply, her face bathed in tears, her eyes locked on Early's across the room. He held his sister's intense stare, felt a strange flux flowing at him and swathing his whole body.

'You gonna be all right, baby!' he told her.

And in his heart, he was surprised to find that he had never had any doubts about it.

Groups of teenagers were lined up on the kerb in front of the low-rise blocks, leaning on cars, talking, smoking, sipping out of brown-paper-wrapped bottles of malt liquor. The area was a bleak vision of old buildings, fenced empty lots and rundown grocery stores and delis. A grubby black man in a dirty overcoat was staggering in the middle of the street, cursing at every passing vehicle though they were doing their best not to run him down. Two young kids holding on to their mother just out of the corner store were looking at him intently. Several pairs of suspicious eyes locked on to the black van as it drove by.

'Place looks tense,' Early remarked as Ice parked farther up the road, in front of the red-painted half-boarded store, engine running.

Booker was watching the row from behind smoked glass.

Less than a minute later, a young man with a blue bandanna and white sweater sauntered across the road to the van.

'What's up, Booster?' Ice asked.

'Cool, Ice.'

The youth was bouncing on the spot as if listening to some slow backbeat inside his head.

'What's up with the homies?'

Booster glanced back.

'Kid from the project got done by some Puerto Ricans on a deal over the line. Things kinda hyped right now.'

Ice nodded.

'What's up with my package?'

'Guy's holed up inside, last block across, first floor, door sixty-six. Came in around five, must be sleeping.'

'He alone in there?'

Booster shook his head.

'No, the girl who lives there's a crackhead. She deals some, so the door keeps knocking, but they all fucked up. No heat on that side.'

'Where's his ride?'

'Parked behind the block. Fucked-up brown Chevy.' Booster added, bouncing and grinning: 'Got two tyres punctured, though. Couldn't leave in a rush.'

Ice nodded, appreciating the work.

'Nice play, homes!'

'Looks like the guy knows he's wanted; paid couple kids on the block to let him know if anybody ask for him,' Booster said.

'Yeah...' If he hadn't had to deal with the matter himself, Ice could have told Booster who the target really was. He wouldn't have left the project alive.

'I take it from there. You and your boy can move out. Check me out later.'

'A'igh'. I be down at the mall if you need me.' Booster moved out.

Ice drove out, went around to enter the project from the far side.

'Got to park round the back, in case we need to haul up the boy...'

They found a brown Chevy, rather beaten looking as described by Booster, in the parking lot by the last block. Ice man-oeuvred the van behind a rubbish chute.

'Right, now we gotta have a conversation with that fugitive cop.'

'How you wanna do that?' Early asked. 'The boy knows he's wanted by the mob, he must be real nervous.'

Ice scratched the stubble on his chin, a sure sign of deep thinking with him.

'Yeah... If we bust in, he's gonna hear it and start shooting. We can't afford to have the cops coming over.'

Early said:

'Well, it's a crack joint; we just knock on the door and ask for a deal.'

He didn't sound like he was joking but Ice smiled.

'Man, you couldn't pass for a crackhead...' He added, motioning to the quiet enforcer watching the derelict blocks through the glass: 'And Booker neither!'

That was true. But then they heard Booker say:

'But she sure can.'

Ice and Early looked to see what Booker was talking about. On the other side of the parking bay, across the waste ground beyond the tall wire fence, a lanky silhouette was heading their way. Judging by her agitated walk, arms moving out of synch with her stride, the woman was in some rush. As she came closer, her yellow top and long black skirt hardly concealed a tall and bony frame, topped by a black face with strikingly large eyes. The girl kept glancing around, like she expected to be jumped on any time or something.

'Yeah, ... and she ain't acting,' Ice remarked.

The pair of sneakers on her feet was well worn and discoloured, her hair plaited in an haphazard way, sticking out in places, adding to her theatrical appearance.

'Your play,' Early told his cousin.

Ice winced. 'I knew you was gonna say that!'

The girl was getting level with the van. Ice lowered his window.

'Yo, girl!' he called out, trying his best to smile at her.

She stopped and turned to see where the voice was coming from, her eyes focusing on the black van. It was clear that she was in a state of mental turmoil, the way she started frowning, crossed her long and bony arms across her chest.

'Excuse me, I just need to ask you something.'

Ice sounded kind and unthreatening, knowing the young woman was worried and afraid at being called by someone she didn't know. She took two steps towards the van, then stopped, unfolded her arms, rubbed her hands on her skirt.

'What's up?' she asked, sounding hoarse and puzzled.

'Don't be afraid, sis; I just want to ask you something,' Ice reassured the girl.

She could have been in her late twenties but her face, dry skinned, washed-out eyes and cracked lips gave her ten years more.

'What is it?' the girl asked, coming a little closer.

'You going up there?' Ice asked.

She could make out Early's face on the other side, but he wasn't looking her way.

'Why?' she asked, squinting like she was trying to establish whether she knew Ice or not.

Like all crack addicts, the girl lived haunted by fear and doubt, always suspecting that someone wanted to harm her. The liberating high from the drug lasted just minutes, only to drop her lower than she had started out before sucking on the glass pipe.

''Cause I need a favour,' Ice lied with an open smile. 'The girl upstairs shacking with a friend of mine and I just want to surprise him.'

'Yeah?'

The girl uncrossed then crossed her arms over her body once more, her brain ticking to try to understand what the man wanted from her. And, more importantly, like all drugheads, what she could get out of it.

'Yeah. All I'd like you to do is to tell my boy someone wrecking his car, so he'll come down and I can surprise him. It's just a joke, you know what I'm saying?'

No argument in the world could have got

through to the girl as fast as the greenback paper. On seeing the note appear in Ice's hand, she suddenly seemed to wake up fully, one hand already halfway to the door of the van.

'I'll do it for you!' she said.

Ice told her:

'Yo, make sure you tell my boy exactly what I'm telling you, right?'

'Yeah, man, I'll tell him.'

'What you gonna say?'

The girl licked her lips like a dog looking at a Kentucky Fried Chicken restaurant.

'Eh, I'll tell him somebody trashing his car, right?' She looked at Ice expectantly.

'Yeah, that's good; tell him you seen some kids trashing a brown Chevy, that one!' Ice was pointing to the car parked a couple of yards away in the bay.

'That's your friend's car?' the girl asked.

'Yeah.'

'It looks like it's been trashed already,' she pointed out.

Ice smiled at the wit.

'Yeah, well; he just likes his car to look bad, so nobody goes for it. But you tell him that anyway. Tell him kids been stealing his wheels when you came up, right?'

'Yeah, man, I'll tell him.'

'Make sure he comes down here.'

'All right... You gonna gimme the money?' The girl's eyes were gazing at the banknote in Ice's hand.

'Sure.'

Ice stretched out his hand. With a speed you wouldn't have thought possible for a shaky-looking crack addict, the girl grabbed the $50 note, her hand closing around it, clutching it tight against her chest like she was afraid Ice might try to take it back.

'OK, I'm going up and telling your friend to come down 'cause kids out here trashing his car, right?' She was already turning on her heels.

'Yeah, right.' Ice nodded. 'And don't make me wait out here, girl. I don't want you to sit down and blow that money on shit while I'm hanging out here.'

The girl stopped.

'No, no. I'm just getting a piece, for my nerves, you know. 'Cause I'm sick. I'm ah keep some money to buy milk for my kids.'

'You got kids?'

She thought about it.

'Yeah, man, I got two boys.'

Ice told her:

'All right, look here; you get my boy to come down here in less than five minutes and I give you another fifty, OK?'

This time her eyes widened, and some kind of sad smile came across her tired features.

'All right. I get him down here real fast.'

'You send him alone, come down a little later.'

'Right, right.' Something was bugging the girl. She asked:

'You want me do anything else for you?'

Ice didn't have time to say 'no' before she offered:

'Another fifty, I could do you something real nice...'

Though he felt like cursing her, Ice knew she was too far gone ever to understand why. He just shook his head.

'Just go up and do the job, that's all I want, all right?'

'Yeah, yeah...Wait out for me.'

The girl hit the stairs as fast as her weak, spindly legs could carry her.

'You think she'll do it?' Early asked.

'The only thing she thinking about right now is that other fifty. Girl all fucked up. Imagine the kids!' Ice sounded disgusted.

'Booker, better get ready for the package,' Early said.

The big man was wearing a white tracksuit and black combat boots. He opened up and got out, already checking out the best spot. A small recess by the bottom of the concrete seemed ideal. Ice wound up his window. They waited.

It took another minute and a half but then a pair of legs in jeans came running down the steps. The man was tall and well built, brown skinned, wearing an open denim shirt over a white vest. His straightened hair sleeked back in a ponytail and a gold stud in one ear, he looked streetwise and stylish. He jumped the last three steps, stopped as his eyes locked on to his car, alone and undisturbed. A puzzled look appeared on his face. Then Ice's window slid down and the man's head jerked towards the van.

'Hey, Jerry! You a hard man to find!' Ice sounded almost happy.

Clocking the two men in the van, Jerry reacted like the fugitive he was. Fast, his hand went to his back, under the shirt, flashed out again holding a mean-looking silver .45.

'Jerry! Take it easy, man, we on your side...' Ice held up his hands, sounding worried at the sight of the gun.

'Who the fuck are you?' Jerry growled, eyes squinting, his brain scanning to try to make out the features of the men in the van. So many enemies he had.

Then, from behind, a deep voice answered his question:

'We your new friends, Jerry.'

He spun around to face it, but the new menace was much too ready and too fast for him. His gun hand didn't complete the half-circle to point at Booker before the big man had already grabbed it and twisted it behind his back. There was a yell of pain, then a dull sound as Booker simply slammed Jerry's face into the iron railings of the stairs. The second scream was much louder than the first.

'Aaah!... My nose...!'

It must have been painful. Jerry's face was now bloodied from his broken nose. His gun was already safely tucked in Booker's own waist. The enforcer mercilessly dragged him to the van, opened the door and threw the cop inside. Inside two minutes of Jerry coming down the stairs, he had disappeared like he'd never been there.

Then someone was coming down and asking:

'You seen him? Where is he?' The pitiful-looking girl had fulfilled her mission and come back for the rest of her pay.

'He's gone down the road to get some drinks. Thanks, he was real happy to see me,' Ice told her.

'You gonna gimme the other fifty?' the girl asked.

Her face and tone of voice spoke of someone used to being deceived and abused. Ice took out another note, a hundred this time.

'Yo, make sure you don't spend it all on that shit. Buy your kids some food, all right?'

The girl rushed to the banknote, grabbed it quickly.

'Yeah, yeah, I'll do it. I look after my kids good, man,' she insisted.

Ice nodded.

'Cool. Later.'

He fired up his engine, moved out without another look at the skinny girl and her washed-out gaze. Glancing back, he saw that Jerry wasn't moving.

'He's having a nap,' Booker told him.

The disused movie theatre had been closed for years. Like many other small movie houses, it had been killed by larger mall entertainment complexes. The boss of the real estate agency owning the place was a long-time school buddy of Ice, always ready to help a friend in need. Today the place was staging a live performance, a private drama.

Early sat on the stage, looking at the fugitive DEA cop asleep, tied up on a chair. His eyes expressed no sympathy. Standing by the chair, Ice called out:

'Wake up that nigger; we got to talk.'

Booker grabbed the man by the collar, hit him twice with his large meaty hands, just enough to bring him to. Jerry snorted, shook and opened his eyes. He looked around, trying to understand where he was. His first question was the same as the last before he went to sleep.

'Who the fuck are you?'

'You asked that before, Jerry,' Ice told him. 'Now listen: you don't know us but we know about you. We've been looking for you.'

Jerry tried to play tough; he was a cop

after all...

'You better cut me loose, you don't know who you fucking with!'

Ice cut him cold:

'We ain't started to fuck with you yet, Jerry, so save your breath. You're here to answer, not to talk.'

Jerry tried to stand up with the chair, his face looking mean. Because he didn't see any weapons, he mistakenly thought he wasn't in much danger. Booker pressed on his shoulder with one hand, slamming him back down.

'You sit down and keep quiet. I won't tell you again.'

Jerry looked at the big man, not much taller than him but somewhat bulkier. His nose hurt like hell, and he recalled how it had happened to him now. But he was a bigmouth, and he had a badge.

'Listen, I don't know what you want but you making a bad mistake. I'm a cop.'

Jerry expected this revelation to impress his hosts. He heard Ice say:

'You not a cop, Jerry, you a bitch ... and that's why we here.'

Something in Jerry's brain clicked. His head was clearing up fast.

'What you talking about?'

'I'm talking about a dirty DEA cop on the run, hiding in a crack joint in the project. I would have loved to give you up to the homies down there, but I need some answers to my questions.'

'Do I know you?' Jerry was looking at Ice.

He didn't do his homework and Ice had always been smart enough to keep out of the limelight.

Ice shook his head.

'That's not what you should worry about right now.' He paused, deciding to make the cop face reality.

'In a way you real lucky, Jerry. We was gonna call Sal in, but we decided it was best to talk with you first.'

A look of genuine fear appeared on Jerry's face.

'You ... you working for Sal?' The voice was much less cocky all of a sudden.

He looked at the three men one at a time. So Sal had anticipated he would hide among his own people and had recruited black guys to track him down ... Jerry felt like his balls were shrinking in his jeans.

'Like I said: you lucky, Jerry.' Ice sneered. 'Now, we ain't got time to rap. You tell us what we want to know and we might just let you go.'

Might as well give the cop some hope. A condemned man always tends to play for time and try to hold back. Hope loosens tongues.

'But if you fuck us around, I'll ask Sal to let me watch him cut your balls off.'

Ice didn't look like a man inclined to joke. The other two neither. Jerry's brain was working fast; he was starting to guess what these guys had come to see him about. Ice's first question confirmed his worst fears.

'Now, tell us what happened the night your DEA friends raided Sal's place.'

In Jerry's mind, the doubt about the black gangsters' connection to him was getting thinner. The query was specific. He didn't want to get these guys angry, especially the shaven-headed, bearded one.

He muttered:

'The raid at Sal's place?'

'Yeah, one of you guys was in there and never made it out, right?'

Jerry's eyes were wide open. These guys were after him for one reason, he realised, and they had precise information. But he made the mistake of trying to play the cop.

'This was a police operation. It's classified.'

'Classified?' Ice raised his eyebrows, a sure sign of rising frustration with him, looked at Early.

For the first time, the young man with the cold face and the dark grey expensive suit spoke.

'Ask him to be truthful.' Early was speaking to Booker.

The enforcer took in the order and before he had time to be afraid Jerry felt the chair he was tied to being lifted up and thrown against one of the round pillars, five yards away. The crash was painful; the chair broke from under him and the rope tying Jerry to it fell loose.

But even if he had wanted to, Jerry couldn't have tried to run. Before he fully realised what had happened, two hands stood him up and Booker started to slap him, methodically, accurately, around the face with his open right hand, then the left, then the right to the ribs, then the left. The big man's face didn't register any effort, or any anger. He just followed Jerry wherever he tried to move to, slapped him relent-lessly, until the pain got him numb and a last hit to the ribcage dropped him to his knees.

'Stop!' he cried. 'Stop! Enough.'

But just like a wound-up robot, Booker didn't seem to hear him. He grabbed him by the collar, yanked him up and delivered another right-hand slap which landed right on Jerry's broken nose. The scream rose in the empty hall. Jerry, feeling he was going to pass out at the next hit, desperately tried to call to the man in the suit who was calmly watching the beating from a distance.

'Please, stop him ... I beg you, man, I'll talk, please,' he yelled.

It seemed Early would never intervene, but eventually he said:

'All right, give him a chance.'

He didn't raise his voice but Booker heard him, stopped with his hand up in the air. Jerry was dragged back all the way to where he first sat, dropped on another chair, untied this time.

'Man, look at you; you all fucked up now!' Ice said.

Jerry looked a mess, blood dripping from his nose and mouth. The worst pain was in his ribs, though. Booker's open-handed slaps had felt like so many hits from a bat. Had he used his fists, the cop wouldn't have survived it. He felt a visceral fear of the enforcer, now standing a little way off, leaning against the wall like he had never left it.

'OK, I'll tell you what you want to know,' Jerry spluttered, his throat dry, lips cracked and swollen.

'Right. From the start, so we won't waste any more time.'

Jerry swallowed painfully.

'I ... I was in business with Sal ... I gave him a deal, some Chinese operators. Sal got them robbed, got twenty Ks of powder.' Jerry paused.

Ice asked:

'The DEA had an operation on Sal, right?'

Jerry sighed heavily, getting his breath back, shook his head.

'No.'

'No?' Ice asked, surprised.

'I just told him we had him under surveillance, that I was gonna cover him.'

Early was listening, knowing Jerry would soon get to the part that interested him.

'So Sal got the drugs'

'Yeah...' Jerry wiped his face with one hand, carefully. 'But he fucked me on the deal.'

'So you tried to bust him?' Ice proposed.

'Yeah ... I knew his uncle, the old man, didn't want him dealing with drugs. If he got busted, he was finished.'

Something occurred to Ice.

'But you wanted to get the drugs too, right?'

Through puffed eyelids, Jerry threw him a pitiful glance.

'He tried to fuck me over... If I busted him, I could keep most of the drugs. He wasn't gonna claim for it in court.'

'Very smart, Jerry.' Ice smirked. 'I always said DEA cops are the most rotten... So what happened?'

Jerry glanced to his right, to Booker, who seemed interested in the story too.

'So we were watching Sal's place, me and my partner...'

'That's the guy who got done...' Ice said.

'Yeah...' Jerry was quiet for a few seconds, as if the mention of his partner's tragic death had got to him. But Ice wasn't into feelings, especially about dirty cops.

'Go on, man!' he said.

'All we had to do was set up a buy on the premises and bust him. I knew Sal had one of his guys dealing for him, he wasn't taking any chances. ... Sal knew me but he didn't know Dick.'

'Dick?'

'Yeah, my partner.'

'Right. Tell me about the girls,' Ice said.

Somehow, Jerry guessed this might be what his problem with these guys was about.

'The girls...' he repeated, kind of sad.

'Yeah. What happened with the girls?'

Jerry paused, just a little, because he knew now Ice wasn't a patient man. He shook his head slowly, defensive.

'I didn't hurt no girl, man. I just wanted to set up Sal, that's all.'

Ice looked straight at the sweaty, broken-up cop.

'Yeah, but then Sal got one of them shot dead.'

'She died?' Jerry asked, looking panicked at the news.

'Sal's hit-man pumped seven bullets into her. Kinda final, right?' Ice remarked, an even colder edge to his voice. 'What happened? Talk, man!'

Jerry closed his eyes briefly then started talking:

'We were watching the place that night, when we saw two girls get inside, pretty girls. Dick said he knew one of them, said he had busted her the year before for trafficking. So we waited, and when they came out we busted them...'

Pause.

'One of them had a half K on her.'

Ice glanced quickly at Early, then asked Jerry:

'You remember their names?'

'Their names?' The question seemed to take Jerry by surprise. He could feel the weight of Ice's eyes. The other two men had their cold gaze on him too.

'Yeah ... yeah; it was, eh ... Inez ... Inez and ... Lisa yeah, that's it.'

Ice waited, watching Early for any reaction, but his cousin's face didn't reveal anything, even to him. One more question was essential:

'Which one was carrying?'

Jerry didn't hesitate on this.

'Inez... She had the shit with her. She was the one Dick knew.'

From the silence that followed his answer, Jerry could sense that something important had been passed on from him to his interrogators, but he couldn't tell what it meant exactly.

Ice said:

'So you busted the two girls and sent them

271

to Sal to bait him.'

'Right,' Jerry confirmed. Blood had started drying around his mouth. 'Dick sent one first ... Inez.'

'She was wired, right?'

'Right. We wired her to get the deal on tape. With that and the girl's testimony in court, Sal was trapped.'

'But it didn't work out...'

Jerry sighed, shook his head gravely.

'No... The girl ... Inez ... she went inside but then the line went dead. We waited about an hour but she didn't come back out.'

'You didn't think about that?' Ice smirked.

'As far as we knew, there was only one exit. And we had her friend...'

'But she messed up your perfect plan.'

'Yeah, she did.'

'Then you sent the other girl in, Lisa?' Ice asked, though it wasn't really a question.

'Yeah, we sent Lisa inside. Dick went with her.'

'What happened then?'

Jerry swallowed, sighed heavily.

'The girl, she was arguing with Dick. She asked him to let her go, she said we had nothing on her...'

The three pairs of eyes were on him, so Jerry couldn't afford too long a pause.

'Dick said she had to set up Sal then she could go ... or he would bust her for the coke. So ... they were inside and...'

It appeared hard for Jerry to go on, so Ice told him:

'I done ask you questions now, this ain't no interview!'

Jerry got the message. He said:

'The girl ... Lisa, she was angry. She said ... she told Dick he was going to pay for that ... and me too. She cursed Dick... Then the line went dead.'

They waited.

'That's all?' Ice asked the cop.

Jerry nodded.

'Yeah, that's all.'

He could see the men were still expecting him to say something.

'That's it, I swear, man! That's the last thing I heard.'

'What did you do after that?'

'I ... I called the office, I told them Dick went in undercover but didn't come out. So we raided the place.'

'But you didn't find anything, right?' Ice asked him.

'No, nothing. We didn't find Dick ... or the girl.'

Down in the office, the mood was tense. Matty was finding it hard to believe Sal's denials. He said:

'Sal, I'll ask you again: did you get Massimo's place blown up?'

The cigarette between Sal's fingers was the fifth one in less than half an hour.

'Look, I'm telling you: I got nothing to do with that, all right?'

Matty had lived through quite a few crises in his years as consigliere to old man Scaffone, but working with Sal had become increasingly difficult. Now he had a major problem on his hands, one that could well sink him and the family for good.

He had always known that Sal was the wrong man to head the family business and had tried explaining that to his old boss at the time. But Giuseppe had lost his only son and his nephew Sal was the only blood candidate he could pass on the hat to. Brash, hot headed and stubborn, Sal was a fatally bad option for the Brooklyn Scaffone family.

'So who else could have done it?'

'I don't know who. That fat asshole Massimo must have many enemies!'

Matty sighed. Even if it was true, all the New York families were going to put it down to Sal. Everyone knew his soldiers had been killed and everyone knew by now that Sal had been messing around with a made man's woman. That was a bad spot to be in. Especially because Sal's bad temper had won him very few friends and lost him many.

'Look, Matty; I know you don't approve of

some things I do, and you think I'm too hot sometimes, but I'm telling you I didn't hit Massimo, all right?' Sal looked straight at the older man, added: 'I would have loved to do it, but it wasn't me. You believe me?'

'OK, Sal, I believe you.'

'OK.' Sal paused, stubbed out his cigarette, asked: 'What do we do now?'

Matty made a face like only older Sicilians can, an expression which only other older Sicilians can read.

'What do we do...?' Matty paused, opened his palms in a gesture of powerlessness.

'We got half the cops in New York watching this place, all our friends are afraid to come for dinner because of it, we losing business and all the other families are smelling blood, waiting for us to fall.'

This was a pretty sober and accurate picture of the situation. And that was exactly what Matty had told Sal's uncle on the phone a couple of hours earlier.

Sal got up, walked to the window, looked through the blinds at the traffic below. It could have been just another Brooklyn Monday. But his closest soldiers were gone, he felt alone and lost. And for the first time in his life, he felt scared.

'We got to find a way out, Matty. There's got to be a way out.'

He turned and came back, asked the consigliere:

'You lived through some tough times, you know how it feels when you're down. Just help me find a way out, sort out all the problems, let's get back to business. I mean, that's what you're good at, right? Finding the best solution when things are bad...?'

Matty kept silent for a few seconds. Then he sighed and said: 'I'm gonna try, Sal, you know I'm gonna try. Just let me think a way out, OK? I need a little time.'

'OK, Matty, you work it out. Just tell me what you want me to do, I'll do it. But get me off the hook, all right?'

Matty nodded slowly.

'OK, you take it easy, Sal. Let me try and see what I can do.' The older man got up, smoothed his shirt out of habit. He left the office.

Alone at his desk, Sal lit up yet another cigarette. In a daze, his mind started drifting back to former days, days when everything was easy and everyone was at his feet. How did things turn so bad, he wondered to himself, where did he go wrong? The ringing of the phone drew him out of his meditation.

'Yeah?... Who's this?'

Someone was on the line talking about things they weren't supposed to know, someone he didn't know!

'Who the fuck are you?' Sal growled, his guts tight inside him suddenly.

Talking to him like he wasn't Sal, the powerful heir to the Scaffone family business, the voice said:

'You keep quiet and listen, 'cause I'll only make you the offer once: you want your friend Jerry the cop? I got him.'

'I don't make no deal with people I don't know,' Sal answered, his tone hard out of habit but feeling as unsteady as he had ever been.

'Well, right now people you don't know are offering you a birthday present. It ain't free, but it'll cost you less than what you're gonna pay if Jerry starts singing to his police buddies about you.'

Sal didn't notice it but beads of sweat were forming around his hairline. He tried to make sense of it all while playing for time.

'How do I know you got Jerry?' he asked.

'How do I know you got the black girl shot and dumped?' the voice asked.

Whoever it was on the other end of the line, they weren't bluffing, Sal was sure of it now.

'Hey, Sal, you fainted or what? Talk, man; I ain't got all night!'

Nobody could have talked to Sal that way just a week ago, but things had turned on him and now he had to play humble or be damned.

'Look, friend, let me talk to Jerry ... so I know he's still alive.'

There was a cold laugh on the line.

'Hey, wiseguy, two things you gotta know: first I ain't your friend, so don't fuck with me; second, Jerry ain't worth shit dead. Now, you wasting my time. I made you an offer but I think you too dumb to realise that!'

'Jerry can say what he wants; he ain't got shit on me,' Sal blurted out in a last attempt at bravado.

The man on the other end sighed.

'Jerry's a piece of shit, but he's still a cop. You wanna take a chance with him testifying his partner went inside your place and never came out? I know you got rid of the body, but it'll be your word against his. And your friend Jerry's gonna charge you with every unsolved crime in the book to get back some credit.'

'Listen, I don't care what you know or what that cocksucker Jerry told you but there's no evidence against me – nothing, you hear? I got the best lawyer in New York, so I'll walk. You can bet on that, you dumb fuck!'

Sal was shouting down the line without realising it. The voice answered, cool and calm.

'Maybe you right, Sal... But ask yourself one thing: is your uncle gonna take the chance of letting you get to court? I know you and him is blood and all that Sicilian bullshit, but maybe he might decide it's better to cut all loose ends than have his business exposed all over the news.' Just a little pause before it added: 'You really think he's gonna back you up on a drug charge?'

Sal was sweating for real now; he could feel his moist hand slipping around the phone.

'OK, OK; look, tell me what you want and maybe you can cut a deal.'

'Right, if it's what you want, but remember I'm doing you a favour.'

'Yeah, right ... so, what about Jerry?'

'Jerry's here with me, all ready for delivery. I'll let you have him for two Ks of your Chinese powder. What happens after is none of my business. You go your way with your package, and I go mine with my present. You want the deal, Sal? Talk fast, you wasted enough of my time...'

Sal's throat was dry, his head feeling dizzy. Jerry gone was the only way to cut himself off from the fateful poison deal, he could see that now.

'Two Ks? You got a deal. Tell me when and where, me and you do business.'

'OK, OK, Sal; you a smart businessman, and you know you get away cheap.'

'Right, let's meet. And no funny tricks, all right.'

The man let out a little laugh.

'You got nothing I want except a little

detergent. And Sal, it better not be detergent!'

'Straight deal, don't worry about that.'

'OK, this is how we gonna do this. You
show up at the old theatre in Flatbush in
thirty minutes, we do the swap. You late ...
forget about it. See you later, Sal.'

The line went dead, and Sal went weak at
the knees. Who the hell was this? And how
the fuck did they know about this cock-
sucking cop Jerry? Fucking molyan! He
should have killed him right after the deal!
That was when all his troubles had started.

In his feverish brain, Sal summed up the
play. Eliminating Jerry would be a great step
towards getting the heat away from him.
The other DEA cop was dead and would
never be found. The girl had disappeared
but somehow Sal didn't think the cops
would find her either. Whoever it was that
had Jerry, two Ks was a small price to pay
for that slimy cop. At last, Sal could see a
light at the end of the tunnel. He picked up
his jacket, buzzed downstairs to call his new
guards and opened the drawer of his desk to
get his private safe key.

A few doors away, Matty put down the
receiver. His furrowed brow showed him to
be deep in concentration. One thing his
many years and long experience of navigat-
ing through the murky waters of mob business had taught him was that, usually, what

is going to happen comes naturally. Wisdom is to take the decision that fortune or fate presents you with. Matty could see that happening now, once more. As he heard the door to Sal's office slam shut, he dialled the Long Island number.

'Hey, Pete, yeah... Let me talk to the boss.'

A little wait, then the voice he knew so well came on. Matty spoke in the old Sicilian dialect for about twenty seconds, summing up what had just happened between Sal and his mysterious caller.

Don Scaffone listened, then once Matty had finished said only one sentence which, even for an Italian listening in, would have sounded like nothing more than an old play-ground saying, like a nursery-rhyme line.

'*Bene*,' Matty said simply, then hung up the phone.

Two changes of cars and some skilful driving from his new driver later, Sal and his three men arrived at the appointed place. He didn't come often to this part of Brook-lyn – this was a downmarket, black-infested area he avoided. But then again, if this was where he had to come to take delivery of the treacherous Jerry, no problem.

On the way down, Sal had been doing some thinking. What he had suspected after the phone call was being confirmed by the neighbourhood his callers selected for the exchange: Jerry was being sold out by his own people. This wasn't really surprising; molyans were known to happily slaughter and betray each other for the slightest thing. The fact that they had asked for two kilos of coke for their brother made Sal smile. Blacks really were a treacherous, cheap and dumb people. To think that some people dared to pretend that the most distant ancestors of Sicilians were black!

In any case, whoever these guys were, they would get a deal today. Jerry was worth much more than two stupid Ks to Sal. In fact, when he thought back, he was convinced it was Jerry, with his scheming, conniving mind, who had convinced Sal to hit the Chinese shipment. Sure it was quick, easy money, but now he realised it had been a rash and foolish move. But after today Sal was sure of what he was going to do, and he wouldn't ever listen to one of them niggers ever again, especially a police one.

'That's the place, down there,' Paolo, Sal's new chief bodyguard, said, pointing to a derelict building next to a drab-looking launderette. To the right was a long and narrow dead-end street.

Women with kids, old, trampish-looking men with bags and loud teenagers walked up and down the busy street. No one seemed particularly interested in one more car parking on the avenue. White men were not common but not an unknown sight either in this part of town. In fact, most of the absentee landlords of this poor neighbourhood were white.

'We're going in through the back,' Sal said.

The four men left the car, entered the alley, walked all the way down. A rusty metal door secured by a rusty lock presented no problem. They filed in, drawing their weapons nervously in the quiet, dimly lit atmosphere of the old movie house.

Through a back room filled with old chairs, bottle crates and wooden folding tables they walked, heading for the light filtering under the door at the far end. Sal was second in line, right behind Paolo. Bertie and Sonny, two new hands, closed the march. Paolo tried the handle; it turned and then the door opened on a half-circle-shaped stage lit by a couple of hanging neon tubes. On the stage, star of the show and prize of the day, a bound and gagged man tied to a chair wriggled when he saw the newcomers.

'Look who's here!' Sal smirked as he walked into the theatre.

The rest of the place, rows of seats rising up from the stage area, was in semi-darkness. Sal walked up to the stage, climbed up while his men scanned the surroundings with squinting eyes, weapons at the ready.

'I've been looking everywhere for you,

Jerry. You got me real worried,' Sal told the tied-up cop, getting close to him.

The muffled sounds and sweat-drenched face and chest of the cop told of his terror.

'You really thought you could fuck me over, eh? You fucking molyan!' Sal cursed the man, slapped him hard around the head.

Before he could go any further, an amplified voice rang out of the old speaker boxes, filling the empty theatre.

'Customers are asked to pay for the goods before handling them.'

Sal and his men jerked around, looking for the source of the unexpected warning. At the top of the gradient, behind the topmost seats, something moved, and they made out a silhouette getting out of the operator room, starting down the steps, slowly.

'You're right, friend, I got to pay you first. Come down here, I got what you want.'

Ice walked all the way down to the second row of seats, taking his time. The four mob guys were watching him, watching his hands easy by his sides. Sal signalled to Sonny, who laid the briefcase on top of the stage of the front.

'Two Ks, like you said. Here it is.'

In his favoured denim shirt and pants, gold chain shining against the tired neon lights, white Kangol furry cap on his head, Ice seemed to have all the time in the world.

'It's real nice of you to have made the trip

from uptown, Mr Sal,' he said, sounding relaxed. 'But you see, I lied to you: it's not the drugs I'm after. Drugs are bad for your health, you must know that.'

Sal didn't like the superior tone of voice or the cool attitude of the young black man. He had no time for games either.

'Look, kid; you asked for two Ks for that piece of shit up there. Here it is. Now, you take it and be nice or you try to be smart and then ... you get nothing. Either way, I'm taking the cop back with me.'

It sounded serious the way Sal had said it. And he meant it too. Things had been rough enough lately; he wasn't about to be fucked around by a black kid. Not today, not ever.

'Hey, Sal, don't be so nervous, man,' Ice replied, very smooth. 'And I don't think it's wise of you to try and threaten me like that. After all, I'm doing you a favour; without me you'd have never found your old friend Jerry.'

Sal held back a little.

'Yeah, you're right, kid. Now what d'you want? You said two Ks, you got it.'

'Like I said, Sal, that's not what I really want.' Ice waited a little, then he said: 'What I really want is you.'

Sal didn't answer right away. His men looked around some more but couldn't see much anyway. The black kid sounded like he was crazy, probably high on drugs...

Then, without warning, true to his rash nature, Sal did something nobody expected. Quickly, he went into his waist, drew the 9mm he liked to keep there and in one fluid move turned around and shot three rapid-fire bullets into Jerry. The echoes of the shots rang in the empty hall for a few seconds.

His smoking gun still in hand, Sal turned back to face Ice. 'Like I said, kid; you get two Ks, or you get nothing. A deal is a deal.'

If Sal expected to have caught Ice short or even impressed him, he was wrong. Cool as if nothing had happened, the young black man looked at him from where he stood and said:

'You know, I knew you was gonna do something like that, Sal.' Then, a little more harshly in tone, he added: 'Now, you all drop your weapons.'

There was a short silence, then Sal let out a little cocky laugh. His men didn't laugh outright but seemed to find it funny too.

'You know something, kid; you should really get off the drugs. It fucks up your mind,' Sal said.

Paolo made a little chuckling sound. Sal shrugged. He felt better already, knowing he had just tied up one of the loose ends that threatened his peace of mind. He looked at Ice.

'You had a chance to get your two Ks, kid, but now I think I might as well take them back. But I'll leave you alive, 'cause I like you, kid.'

Ice didn't reply. Sal said:

'Now I got things to do. See you around, kid.'

Just as Sal was finishing his sentence, Ice simply raised his right hand and the theatre suddenly lit up like a football stadium on Superbowl night. The powerful glare of floodlights directed straight at the stage hit the four mob guys. And immediately after, they heard the unmistakable sound of automatic weapons and pump-action shotguns being armed.

'I asked you all to drop your weapons once already,' Ice said very drily. 'You got three fucking seconds.'

Sal was not stupid enough to do or say anything different. He and his men dropped the handguns on the theatre floor as if the metal had suddenly got red hot. From behind the seats where they'd been crouching, O, Danny, G-man and James looked at the four disarmed mobsters below them. One word from Ice and they would have happily replayed the St Valentine's Day massacre in the old movie house.

A little higher up, to the right, Early watched from the seat he had never left. Right behind him sat Booker's big frame.

Ice came down a little, stopped in front of Sal.

'You're not very bright, Sal, that's why you got yourself in such deep shit,' he declared. 'I know you wonder what we really want with you, and I'm gonna tell you, 'cause every man go the right to know the truth before he dies.'

Sal found that he felt sweaty suddenly. He glared at the black man, the one he had so foolishly taken for a pushover. The three Italian guards were trying to make themselves invisible, but in vain.

'Whatever you and that cop here did, I don't give a fuck... But you made a mistake, man; a girl, a young girl, put her life on the line for you, 'cause she wouldn't give you up to the cops. And to thank her, you got her shot!'

Ice stopped, leaving Sal the time to take in what he had just revealed to him. Then he motioned to Early up there, very quiet and still.

'She was his little sister,' Ice said.

Early slowly got up, walked down the steps, dignified in his suit and light blue silk shirt. Booker moved right after him, his extra-large faithful shadow. When Early got to within a couple of yards of Sal, he stopped and looked him straight in the eye.

'My name is Early Hanley,' he said calmly. 'I just wanted you to know that, before you die.'

The move Early made to take out the

weapon was so swift, so unexpected for someone walking and speaking so slowly, that not even Ice saw the whole of it. But within three seconds, a long and thin blade with a grey pearl handle had appeared in his left hand. Sal had no time to be more afraid than he already was, but he could already feel it in his guts.

But then, before Early did anything else, something happened that no one present in the room, black or white, had expected.

'Hold on, please, wait, wait...'

They all turned to the side door to watch a short little rotund man hurrying towards them. He seemed almost out of breath, looking very strange in his dark grey long coat and hat.

Ice frowned; Early stopped where he was; Booker moved slightly forward to cover him, just in case. But the little fat white man had his hands out, empty, and his pinkish round face looked anything but threatening. His voice was high and comical when he spoke.

'I'ma late, I'm sorry. Hey, Sal!'

Sal looked at the man as if he had seen Jesus himself come down from his cross, stunned. When he recovered, he said:

'Rafe, what you doing here?'

He couldn't quite understand how the man had found him, but Sal was feeling immensely grateful and happy to see him here at this precise moment. The three guards were as still as statues. O and his crew had their guns ready but waited on Ice. And Ice wasn't moving.

But Rafaele, Bambino as they called him, seemed more interested in Early than in Sal. He said:

'Eh, mister, I don't know you but ah ... please, forgive my friend here, he's a little crazy but his uncle, eh, he send me to look after him.'

In the heavy Italian accent, the speech sounded weird and almost funny. But Early wasn't smiling. He didn't care who the fat and short white man was or what he was here for; this was his moment.

He said:

'Look, man, I don't know you and I have no problem with you...'

Bambino was listening, his face open as he looked up at the elegant young black man.

'...but I have a personal score to settle with your friend Sal, so I'll ask you once to keep out of it.'

Early's tone was firm but polite, too polite maybe. Bambino didn't seem to notice the long blade in his hand, but he could read the determination in his eyes.

He said.

'Eh, please, tell me, what is this problem you have with Sal? Maybe we can talk, you know, work it out. Please, tell me.'

Even Early was finding it hard to disrespect the little Italian, even though he was
a man of few words and knew he would get
what he had come for. He told the short
man:

'There's nothing to talk about, mister, it's
personal.'

Early paused, then added, looking straight
at Bambino: 'Sal killed my sister.'

That news seemed to go straight to Bambino's heart. He seemed surprised, then
shocked, turned to Sal and asked him:

'Sal, you killed his sister?'

Sal told himself Bambino was buying him
time, trying to get him off the hook. Not
showing enough regret, he said:

'Hey, look: I didn't know it was his sister,
OK?' Bambino turned back to Early, looking up to face the taller black man. He said,
opening both hands in a gesture of apology:

'He didn't know. He's sorry. His uncle, he
told me to bring him home ... he needs to
talk to him.'

Early's face showed no feelings, nothing,
but he had spent a whole week searching for
Sal, so he wasn't inclined to patience.

'I'm only gonna tell you this once, so listen
up: Sal is a dead man. But no one else got to
die here. You and your friends are free to go.
Now, if you really love Sal that much, tell
me and I'll ask my boys to make it quick for
you.'

Bambino listened, his blue eyes on Early's. There wasn't anything to be negotiated, he could see that. But, unexpectedly, he started to smile. A large, open and almost childlike smile.

'Hey, look: I understand. Sal did you wrong, and you have the right to take his life. But me, I don't want to die for Sal.'

The condemned man threw a bewildered look at Bambino. What the hell was he saying? Worse, Bambino then turned to him and declared, sounding totally unconcerned:

'Sal, your uncle, he send me to help you but it looks like I come too late. You made a lot of trouble. Now this man is gonna kill you, I can't do nothing for you.'

This wasn't possible! Sal kept thinking Bambino had a plan, some kind of last play to save him. But up there in the stands, four guns were trained on him and his friends and, hard as he tried, he just couldn't see a way out. He said:

'OK, listen, mister ... Hanley, right? I know I did wrong but it wasn't personal. I was just trying to protect myself from the cops... You can understand, right? I mean ... there must be a way we can work it out, right?'

'Wrong.' Early stared at the mobster with visible contempt. 'Only your blood can buy back my blood.' A cold sentence that drop-

292

ped in the quiet theatre like steel on a marble floor.

'Rafe, do something!' Panic was in Sal's voice now. But Bambino shrugged helplessly. 'It's the price of blood, Sal.'

He turned to Early:

'I understand, mister; we do the same thing back in Sicily.'

Then, apparently out of context, he said:

'Hey, that's a nice knife you got.' He had just seemed to notice Early's blade. 'Can I see it?'

Early heard it but thought maybe the fat Italian man was crazy. But then Bambino said again: 'I had a knife a little like that, before, you know. Please, just for a minute, mister. I'm sorry, can I look at it?'

Not many things could catch Early unawares, but this strange request in the present situation was really bizarre. He looked the white man in the eyes. Next to him, Booker was watching, puzzled but alert. He didn't know why he did it, but Early raised the knife, a present from his late father, and handed it to Bambino, handle first.

The white man smiled kindly.

'Thank you, mister, just a minute.' Then he looked at the knife, admiring the handle, sizing the long thin steel blade, nodding like an expert.

'It's a beautiful knife, beautiful.'

Nobody present quite saw the beginning of it, but one second Bambino was running the blade flat on his little fat hand, the next it was embedded to the hilt in Sal's chest. The mafioso gasped one last time, his eyes widened in shock, then he dropped to the floor. The three guards had not moved a muscle. They knew better.

No one made a sound or a move for at least a minute. Just as quickly as he had stabbed Sal in the heart with it, Bambino pulled the blade out. Then, as naturally as if he had just swatted a fly, he took out a white handkerchief from his coat pocket with his free hand and carefully placed the red-stained blade on it. Then, with the same little smile as when he had asked to borrow it, he handed it back to Early, handle first.

'A beautiful knife, mister, beautiful.'

Both men stared at each other for what seemed like a long, intense moment. Then Bambino said, in his little squeaky voice:

'Now you got Sal's blood. I keep the body, all right?'

Early nodded slowly.

'All right,' he said simply.

Tuesday

Marylee's aunt was short, plump and cheerful; an energetic little lady with glasses and a head of grey hair. A widow, she had been a schoolteacher all her life and now divided her retirement gracefully between church activities and a couple of old friends from the neighbourhood. The area of Trenton she lived in, just on the outskirts of town, breathed tranquillity, with nice little cottages with lots of shrubs and potted plants and still-friendly community police officers.

'Have some more of the cake, child,' Aunt Belinda told her niece.

'It's all right, Auntie, I had some already.'

'Have another slice.' Marylee's aunt peered at her from behind her glasses. 'Look at you, you all bones! A woman in your condition have to eat more.'

Marylee was starting to wonder whether she should have told Aunt Belinda about her pregnancy. She'd been fussed over like she was a sickly child. To placate the woman, she picked up another slice of the sponge cream cake, bit off a small piece and smiled at her aunt.

'I promise I will get to be two hundred pounds by next month, Auntie,' she declared.

Aunt Belinda shook her head, moved out of the kitchen muttering something about young women and troubled times.

Early was on the phone to Miami in the living room next door. They'd come early to check on Lisa but she was still asleep. Marylee said it was a good sign; the more rest the injured young woman got the quicker her body would recover. Also, she explained to Ice and Early that Lisa's spirit would nourish itself in dreams and help her overcome her ordeal. Apparently, Dr Willard's theory had convinced her and she was becoming something of an expert in psychosomatic matters. Ice had gone out too, taking Booker with him.

'Everything all right?' Marylee asked, as Early came back to sit at the table.

'Yeah. I found out what I needed to know.'

Marylee watched while Early poured himself some more tea, dropped two sugars into the cup. He seemed to have things on his mind. Ice had given her only a brief outline of the events of the previous day, and she knew better than to ask too many questions about her husband's business in general. This was a family affair, and she was part of the family.

Early sipped some tea, looked up.

'What's up?' he asked.

'You know where the money is?'

Early put down the cup, sat back and sighed.

'Yeah.' He nodded.

He could see Marylee wanted to be told but knew better than to push for the story. Yet, sometimes, even he needed to talk.

'Lisa's cousin got it.'

'What?' Marylee frowned, puzzled.

Early explained:

'The girl Lisa was with ... Inez, her name is, she's Lisa's cousin.'

He could see Marylee was lost there, so Early added:

'On her mother's side.'

There was a pause as the young woman tried to make sense of it. She said:

'But, I thought the girl was ... Hispanic...?'

Early nodded.

'Yeah, she is. She's Colombian.'

That didn't make any sense at all to Marylee.

'I'm gonna tell you the whole story,' Early said. He still seemed deep in thought, not angry but rather sad. He started:

'About twenty-five years ago, my father started out in Miami. Back then, him and his people were trying to set up a base and make some money, but the business down there was controlled by the Latinos, especially Cubans and Colombians. It was war on the street, because the Jamaicans decided they should run the areas where their people lived. At some point, things got so hot that the police was cramping down on everybody because there was too much killing going on. So my father went to meet a big Colombian boss and managed to work out a deal to buy directly from him. After that, things worked better and everybody was doing good business.'

Marylee was listening, interested. She asked:

'That's the time Ice's mother came up from Jamaica?'

'Yeah, my father brought Aunt Jennifer up from Yard but things around him were too hot so he decided to send her to New York to stay with some relatives. She liked it better up there... Then he brought our mother from Jamaica. Wally was like two years old at the time. I was born the next year, but after a while, Mama decided she preferred to go back home. I think things were already difficult between them. She couldn't take the kind of life her husband was living, I guess. She wanted to take us back but our father said it was better for us to go to school in Miami, so she left us down there.'

'He raised you alone?'

Early shrugged.

'We had relatives in Miami, so they looked

after us. The old man was often out there on the street, but he made sure to come and see us every day. He was always nice to Wally and me, he was a good father.'

Early seemed lost in memories for a little while. Marylee asked:

'So, what about Lisa?'

'Lisa … yeah…' Early paused again, then went on: 'It must have been a year or two after Mama went home, our father took us on a drive one day and brought us to a house in a different part of Miami. We were just kids, it's only later he explained all that to us. So, that day we went there and there was this woman, a young woman, very pretty. Her name was Carmen, and she was very nice to us. We went out and bought clothes and toys. I remember she bought us ice cream and things. Then we went home… We never saw her again… That was Lisa's mother.'

'Really?' Marylee asked.

'Yeah,' Early confirmed. 'I only learned the whole story later, much later. She was the daughter of the big man our daddy was doing business with.'

'The Colombian?'

Early nodded. 'Yeah.' He shook his head, smiling a little. 'Our daddy was always nice with women. But this time, he went too far. You can imagine: the daughter of some big rich Colombian don … with a black man?'

Marylee made a face that said she understood what Early meant.

'What happened then?'

'Well, Lisa was born the following year.'

'And her mother?'

Early shook his head.

'Things weren't cool with the family. You know how Colombians are; they're very racist when it comes to their women. When she told them she was pregnant by our father, Lisa's uncles wanted to kill him, but her father said he didn't want that. The old man went to see him and said he loved Carmen and wanted to marry her. Apparently, Carmen's father had nothing against him personally, but in his position he couldn't agree to that. When Lisa was born, her family wanted her to leave the child with us and go back to Colombia but she refused to leave her child or her man.'

'So, how did it work out in the end?'

'In the end? Badly … Carmen's family kidnapped her one day and shipped her back to Colombia, with Lisa … she was about three months old. There was nothing our father could do. But one of Carmen's sisters liked him and she used to pass on information to him, send him pictures of Lisa. Then, about ten years later, she sent a message telling him Carmen was dead. She said she had a car accident.'

'Oh my God!'

Early sighed.

'Yeah... But her sister kept in contact, and a couple of years later she convinced the grandfather to let Lisa return to Miami. That's when she came to live with us.'

Marylee couldn't believe this. She asked:

'So that girl, Inez...'

'She's one of Carmen's sister's children. But Lisa never said she kept in contact with her. She knew I wouldn't like it.'

'It's her family,' Marylee pointed out.

Early looked at her.

'You can never trust these people; they have no word. They'll sell out anybody, even their own. All Latinos are like that.' He stopped, then added: 'You see what happened to Lisa.'

Marylee thought Early was probably right in his judgment. She was silent for a moment, reflecting on the story she'd just heard. Lisa never talked about her mother, it seemed. She asked:

'And Ice knew all this?'

Early said:

'Ice is my blood. But I asked him not to tell anybody.' Then he added: 'But now you're gonna give him a baby; you're one of us too.'

'That's where he lives?' Booker asked.

Ice nodded.

'Nice house, eh?'

'You sure he's in?'

'Yeah, I called at the precinct for him. They said he went home.'

From the van, they watched the pretty little cottage atop a low rise, with the red-tiled roof and driveway bordered by evergreens. The car was parked outside, so Burrows intended to go back out.

'You wanna come up?' Ice offered.

Booker declined. 'I'll wait for you.'

'I won't be long. I just need to check something.'

Booker asked:

'You trust that cop?'

'Let's say I know what he won't do. A cop who doesn't take money is the best kind.'

Booker looked like he could see Ice's point.

'Right,' he said.

'Soon come.'

Ice got out, walked across the road. He passed the gate, walked up to the door and rang the bell. A check from the other side, then the key turned and Burrows' face appeared, surprised but not angry.

'How d'you find me?' he asked.

'Wasn't too hard. Now we both know each other's address.'

Burrows said:

'You should have been a cop... Coming in? I'm finishing lunch.'

Ice entered the house, neatly decorated,

with nice carpet on the floor and peach-coloured walls. The kitchen was small but bright and well furnished.

'I thought you said you were divorced...' Ice remarked.

'I am... That don't mean I got to live in a dump,' the policeman answered, sitting back down at the breakfast bar in front of his plate.

'Want some?' he offered.

'Cool. I had breakfast on the way.'

'Some beer in the fridge...'

Ice decided it was a genuine offer, and him and Burrows were cool anyway. He picked up a Miller and sat across from the eating man.

'FBI called me this morning. Looks like Sal got away from them after all...' Burrows said between two bites.

'Gone to a higher court,' Ice offered laconically.

'I like that.' Burrows smiled, swallowed. 'I got a call to the scene last night... Not pretty.'

Ice could feel the cop watching him.

'Yeah? I heard he got killed by a cop.'

Burrows wiped his mouth, sipped from his beer bottle.

'Apparently, he met with the DEA guy who set him up. Looked like they killed each other over some drug deal. Very messy. The cop shot to death, Sal stabbed up in the

303

chest; the place was like a butcher shop.'

'The wages of sin.' Ice shrugged, sipped some cold beer.

'Yeah.' Burrows nodded. 'Works out all right for you.'

'Me?'

'Yeah. I mean, no Sal, no need for a witness any more. Lisa's free now.'

Ice seemed to think about it. No sense playing dumb any more, the score had been settled. He told Burrows:

'She was the only innocent one.'

'Hmm... I hope she gets better.'

'She's strong... And we'll keep praying for her.'

'Good.' Burrows stretched.

Outside, through the garden bay window, a few clouds in an otherwise blue sky; the promise of a warmer spring already had the early buds showing colour.

'What about you?'

'Me? I'm all right.'

'Got any plans?'

Ice found it funny that the man should ask him that; he had been doing a lot of thinking and, yes, he had some plans.

'I might take a vacation,' he said. 'I need some time off.'

'We all do sometimes... Where you planning on going ... the Caribbean?'

'Maybe ... but I got to go west first.'

'Cali, eh?'

'Yeah, my wife ain't seen her family in a while. I thought I'd go along.'

'Good idea... Ever been there?'

Ice drank some of the Miller, shook his head.

'Can be rough down there too ... beautiful, but rough, in places.'

'Hey, I'm going on vacation. I'll be like a tourist.'

Burrows smiled.

'When you're born and raised in Brooklyn, you're a tourist anywhere!'

They laughed at the remark.

'Anyway, I just came by to check you out. I'm going back home now.'

'Back to the old turf.'

'Yeah.' Ice nodded. 'But maybe Cali will appeal to me, you never know.'

'Thinking of retiring, Ice?' Burrows squinted.

'Thinking about a lot of things lately. Maybe I need to change certain things ... I guess we all feel like that at times.'

'Change is the essence of life,' Burrows said, like it was a wise thing to say.

Ice nodded.

'Yeah... Sounds true.' He asked: 'What about you: ever feel like a change?'

Burrows thought about it, said:

'Sure. But who's gonna take care of the streets? They need someone like me, someone who's not just there to shoot people or send them to jail.'

'I never thought about it like that but you're right.' Ice got up. 'I'll see you around.'

'I guess you will.' Burrows walked Ice to the door. When he was out on the porch, he said:

'Tell Early to stay safe now.'

'You got it.'

Ice made a salute, turned and walked back down the way he had come.

Burrows waited until he had passed the gate, then closed the door, his face serene.

Wednesday

The road to JFK was busy as always but there was no rush – they had left in plenty of time.

Booker for one was impatient to get back to Florida. It had only been a week but already he felt homesick. A man of habit, he never liked to leave his home too long. Next to him, Lisa seemed to be looking at the traffic through the glass. Marylee was holding her hand, like she wanted to transmit her own warmth and life energy to the injured girl. She would get better, everyone now was sure of it. That the girl had recovered this much a short week after her terrible ordeal was already a miracle. With care and loving and sunshine to warm her body, she was going to heal fast, that was what Early had told her this morning before they left Ice's house.

'She's in Fort Lauderdale?' Ice asked.

'Yeah... She must have got scared the DEA cop come after her,' Early said.

'The money?'

Early nodded.

'I got my people down there watching her. Looks like she's spending fast.'

Ice thought about it, then remarked:

'The girl really thought she could get away with it!'

'She almost did,' Early answered.

After a pause, Ice asked him:

'You gonna go after her?'

'It's not my business any more; I'll let her family deal with it.' Then he added, as if talking to himself: 'If they wanted to fuck me up, it was a perfect plan.'

Ice thought about it.

'You think the Colombians set it all up?'

'No, they're not that smart. It's just one of them things ... it's like fate.'

It reminded Ice of something.

'You still see it as a sign, right?' he asked.

Early didn't answer right away. His eyes were looking far off through the windscreen when he explained:

'I'll tell you a story... The day Wally get shot, he was suppose to meet a man he had static with in Orlando. That day his driver crashed the car coming to pick him up. The driver was just shaken but the car was mash up. Wally said he had to go anyway, so he borrowed his friend's car. He asked me to drive him up there. Just before we left, his baby mother called and said the youth was sick with fever and she wanted him to come and take them to the hospital. But Wally insisted on going to Orlando, told her to get a taxi. On the way there, we got stopped by police. They searched the car, searched us but didn't find nothing, though Wally had his piece in the trunk...'

Early paused then turned to look at his cousin.

'Lots of signs in life... A man who want to live long better learn how to read them.'

Ice's phone rang; he checked the caller before answering.

'Yeah ... hm ... damn shame ... yeah, cool... Right now I'm on my way to the airport ... yeah, I'll tell him... You call me back later, we'll have a meeting. All right.'

He switched off, looked at Early.

'Danny said to tell you he'll call you in Miami soon.'

After negotiating a change of lane, he added, too casually:

'Oh yeah, our friend West had a terrible

accident last night. His car ran off the road, crashed out and blew up. Looks like West was drunk or something, must have lost control.' Ice shook his head, sighed. 'Fate, I guess... Rest in peace.'

Early took in the news in silence. To him it meant two things: Stan got his call and Danny just got drafted into the family business. He told Ice:

'Looks like you can ease off the street now...'

Ice didn't reply right away.

'I been thinking about a lot of things lately too. Maybe time has come for certain changes, I don't know...'

In the back, Marylee had been quietly listening to the two men. She chose this moment to speak:

'You got to start thinking about your son, give yourself a chance to see him grow up.'

'How you know it's a son?' Ice asked without looking at her.

'I know, that's all.'

Marylee found unexpected support from Early:

'All we try to achieve is for the children; that's what a man's life is about.'

'Yeah, it's true. Like I said: I've been thinking about all that.'

'You know, a lot of people said a lot of things about my father, but I knew him better than anybody,' Early said. 'All he wanted was for us to have things easier than he did. He had no education but he made sure I went to college, so I could know the system from inside.' He added after a short pause: 'And I know he used to pray. Most men people say are bad men pray, you know.'

'Yeah, you got to have sins to be forgiven to really know what prayer means, that's what I think.'

Ice realised after saying this that he had never consciously thought about it, it just came out.

'"Let thy work appear unto thy servants, and thy glory unto their children." I used to hear the old man say that often. I found out later it comes from Psalm Ninety. I didn't know he still read his Bible,' Early said with a little smile.

Then he heard Marylee's voice behind him complete:

'"And let the beauty of the Lord our God be upon us; and establish thou the work of our hands upon us..."'

The iron-barred gate hissed as it slid across the entrance to the domain. For domain it was – swimming pool, gymnasium, tennis courts, movie viewing room, shooting gallery, even horse stables among lawns, gardens, orchards, small ponds and fountains. Skilful and somewhat tasty landscaping concealed the fact that the property could easily turn into a fortified and defendable fortress, should the occasion require it...

The vehicle had been checked through the closed-circuit TV and cleared. Early had only been there once before, invited to Enrique's wedding. Even then he had hesitated; he was in business with the Colombian but he didn't see him as a friend. But then he went, out of courtesy, and the wedding was grand, expensive, food and drinks provided on a lavish scale. Like all rich Hispanics, Enrique tended to be extravagant and flaunt his wealth. The young woman he had married was also from a powerful Colombian land-owing family, of course; in these circles, love, money and blood were always closely related.

Today, the occasion of Early's visit was somewhat less festive. He had wanted to come over straight on arrival from the airport, deal with the problem right away. Denton had come to pick them up in the big Toyota customised minibus Early used to take the family on weekend excursions once in a while, to accommodate Lisa's wheelchair. Denton's horrified look when he saw Early's sister at the airport said it all, and the man kept glancing in the rear-view mirror from time to time, shocked. Early hadn't said much during the trip, just asked

Denton a couple of questions after listening to the man's report of the past week's activities.

The tarmac road leading to the mansion was manned by mean-looking guards, probably the 'peones' Enrique liked to recruit in the back country around Cali, his own town. He seemed only to trust that kind of personnel, brutish and backward types who took orders only from him and obeyed his every wish without any hesitation. Denton parked in front of the large veranda, got out to open up for Early. Booker followed his boss up the steps, glancing back at the three big guys in new bright-coloured shirts the same way they looked at him. Enrique appeared, smiling, wearing one of the white Spanish-type suits he favoured. Carlos, calm as ever, could be seen in the background near the large marble interior stairwell.

'Early, my man!' Enrique beamed like he was welcoming his long-lost blood brother.

'How you doing, Enrique?' Early sounded a little more reserved in his greeting.

'Pretty good, I'm doing OK, my friend.' He patted Early's shoulder, ignored Booker behind him. 'How was New York?'

'Same big old apple,' Early answered, following Enrique into the huge living room.

To the right, through the tall open bay windows, a table was dressed, three beautiful women and another moustached man

Early didn't know sitting there. Carlos nodded at Early.

'Hey, Carlos,' Early said.

Booker rapidly scanned the surroundings, keeping a little way back but not too far.

'You just in time for lunch, amigo. You like salmon? I got some imported from Canada. It's wonderful.'

Enrique seemed in a very good mood or maybe just very high.

'Thanks, but I really don't feel hungry,' Early declined as politely as possible. 'I came straight from the airport.' He paused, then added: 'I said I would get back to you in a week.'

From somewhere in the house, a sentimental Spanish voice crooned.

'You're a man of your word, Early; I like that,' Enrique said.

Early nodded and declared:

'Back home, they say a good name is better than pocket money.'

That made Enrique's smile widen.

'Pocket money, yeah, that's good!' He seemed to find the saying amusing, looked at Carlos, who made a face that said he liked it too. Then Enrique asked:

'So … you got my … pocket money?'

His dark eyes were on Early's, expectant.

But Early shook his head slowly.

'No, Enrique, I haven't got it.'

'No?'

Enrique raised his eyebrows, not yet worried but already less jovial.

'But I know who got it,' Early added.

The Colombian glanced at Carlos, then asked Early:

'What? What you talking about?'

'Don't get nervous, Enrique,' Early said calmly. 'I said I know who got it.'

The two men looked at each other, Early composed and straight faced, Enrique feeling his good mood dissolving. Then Early explained:

'I was going to get it for you ... but then I thought maybe you'd prefer to deal with it yourself.'

It really didn't make any sense to Enrique, what Early was telling him. He looked away towards the table and his guests, ran his hand over his chin, like he was thinking about all this. When he finally spoke, his tone was not quite cold yet but getting there.

'You know something, hombre: I like games too. Sometimes I play with cars, with women ... but I never play with money, you get that?'

Early let him finish.

'I gave you seven days, OK? Today is the deadline; so I tell you again, you get my money, you bring it to me, today! *Entiendes?*'

The atmosphere was a little tenser now, with Carlos watching Early's reaction, Booker watching Enrique but also the guards hanging out on the veranda. Early didn't seem intimidated by Enrique's hostile mood.

'Calm down, *hermano*,' he said. 'Look; I know you want your money, I can see it means a lot to you, so let's keep things simple.'

Early paused; he could feel Carlos watching him, wondering. He offered:

'I give you a name ... and if you say I take care of it myself, I go and do it, today, OK?'

Enrique still seemed totally pissed off, like Early had spoiled his day. He watched him take out a pen and calling card from his jacket pocket, write something on it.

'That's who got your money, Enrique.'

Early handed Enrique the card, watched closely as the Colombian read the name. Two steely black eyes looked up from the card, locked on to Early's face.

'What's up with you, Early, you take some shit and it mess your head up?' Enrique's voice carried not anger but something much deeper, much more lethal. But Early simply pointed out:

'I never touched shit in my life.' He motioned towards the card in Enrique's hand. 'That's the person who you must ask for your money.'

Though Enrique didn't know Early as a man inclined to joke when it came to business, he just couldn't grasp what he was telling him.

'I don't understand what you're talking about,' he said, sounding annoyed now.

Now it was Early's turn to become cold.

'You don't understand?' he asked, squinting at the Colombian standing there with his hands on his hips. 'OK, then I'll show you what I'm talking about. Come on!'

Early turned and started back towards the veranda.

'Come on, Enrique; I'm gonna show you what I'm talking about. Come on!'

Enrique frowned, looked towards Carlos, then followed Early out. Booker watched Carlos, who looked at him, then both also walked after Enrique. Early had already signalled to Denton, standing guard by the minibus, to open the back door. The panel slid open and into view came Lisa and her wheelchair.

'You look at that and tell me if you understand what I'm talking about, Enrique,' Early said very coldly. Enrique had his eyes fixed on the young woman strapped in the metal chair. Carlos had come up and was looking at her too.

'Do you understand now, hombre?' Early asked again, standing by the open door.

Enrique looked like he was in shock for a few seconds. Then he took a couple more steps, stopped a few yards from the minibus.

'You remember Lisa, Enrique,' Early

called out to him. 'Look at her ... look at your little cousin!'

'*Madre de Dios!*' he heard Enrique say finally, watched him bite his fist.

'Yeah...' Early nodded, repressed fury seeping through his words. 'She would like to tell you how it happened, Enrique, but she can't... She can't talk ... and she can't walk either. Maybe she'll stay like that for the rest of her life.'

Enrique bit his lip, asked with a changed voice:

'Who did that?'

Early shook his head, sighed deeply before answering.

'I took care of the people who did that.' He allowed a pause, then told Enrique straight:

'I'll let you ask your sister how it happened.'

Enrique stopped looking at Lisa to ask him, sounding like he was repressing rising anger:

'You're saying this is down to Inez?'

'Your sister got her in a trap, then she ran out on her, left her in a hole. But before she ran out of New York, she made sure she took Lisa's money.'

Early waited but Enrique said nothing in reply. He added:

'Why don't you start by looking in Fort Lauderdale?'

Then he motioned Denton, who closed the sliding door and jumped in behind the wheel. Booker waited for Early to get inside before he did. From the passenger seat, Early called out to Enrique:

'And, hombre: it's over. Over and out, you understand?'

There was no answer from the Colombian. Early didn't expect any.

'Let's go home,' he said.